Puffin Books
Editor: Kaye Webb

D0510094

Danny Fox at the Palace

The smallest fox in the world woke up and found herself alone. She was Danny Fox's newest cub. He and her mother, Mrs Doxie Fox, had gone out to search for food, leaving her asleep. But she woke and left the safety of their den. It was her first adventure and it would have been her last if Danny Fox had not rescued her by one of his clever tricks.

This is the third book about the cunning and wily Danny Fox, who plays tricks on other animals and people – usually to protect his family or friends. His greatest friend, the princess, whose marriage to the fisherman he arranged long ago, has been put into a dungeon by her stepmother, the queen, who wants her to be a 'proper' princess, to live in a grand palace and wear smart clothes.

Danny is longing to rescue her, but can't think of the right trick, until Shaggy, the wise old wild cat, sets him a riddle. Danny solves the riddle and with the help of his grown-up sons Lick, Chew and Shallow. and of the baby, newly named Choke, he sets the princess free.

Funny and adventurous, this new Danny Fox story, published here for the first time, will give pleasure to many admirers, old and new.

Illustrated by Gunvor Edwards

Danny Fox
at the Palace

David Thomson

Puffin Books

Puffin Books,
Penguin Books Ltd,
Harmondsworth, Middlesex, England
Penguin Books Inc.,
7110 Ambassador Road, Baltimore, Maryland 21207, U.S.A.
Penguin Books Australia Ltd,
Ringwood, Victoria, Australia
Penguin Books Canada Ltd,
41 Steelcase Road West, Markham, Ontario, Canada
Penguin Books (N.Z.) Ltd,
182–190 Wairau Road, Auckland 10, New Zealand

Published in Puffin Books 1976
Copyright © David Thomson, 1976
Illustrations copyright © Gunvor Edwards, 1976

Made and printed in Great Britain by
Richard Clay (The Chaucer Press) Ltd, Bungay, Suffolk
Set in Monotype Bembo

Contents

To
Timothy, Luke and Benjamin

1. Danny Saves the Baby Fox

Once long ago when his children were small Danny
Fox was trapped by wolves in the forest, far away on
the other side of the mountain. He lived on the side
nearest the sea but now he had only Mrs Doxie Fox
and their new baby with him in the den. Their older
children, who were called Lick, Chew and Swallow,
were grown up and had left home. The baby was a
little vixen, their first girl. One day, soon after the
baby was born Danny walked out of his den and instead of running off down the mountain path as he
usually did he stood stock still. There was a nasty
smell in the air, and looking up at the sky he saw
black clouds which did not look like clouds at all.
The smell was sharp and made him sneeze. He was
afraid of it and tried, as he always did when he was in
danger, to think of a trick. But he thought, 'Tricks
against wolves are possible. I escaped from them by

tricks. But who can play a trick against the wind?'

He went rather slowly down the mountain path sniffing the horrible air until he saw another fox. Then he stood still, with his long smooth nose with its beautiful black tip stretched out before him and his long bushy tail with its beautiful white tip stretched out behind. The other fox was growling and the hair on its back stood up on end. Then the other fox began to wag its tail. The hair on its back became smooth again and it walked towards Danny in a friendly way. At last Danny knew who it was. It was his own son Swallow, who was now grown up and almost as big as him.

They licked each other's faces and again they smelt the air.

'That is the smell of burning wood,' said Swallow. 'Can't you remember how the farmer at the bottom of our mountain trims his hedges and makes a bonfire of the twigs?'

'It's the same smell,' said Danny. 'But there are no trees on the mountain. And there are black clouds in the sky of a kind we have never seen before.'

'The farmer's bonfire makes little clouds,' said Swallow, 'which soon blow on the wind away. And Lady Shiny the farmer's cat walks off. This is a great big bonfire, burning miles from here.'

'It is the forest!' said Danny. 'The forest is on fire.'

'The forest where the wolves live!' Swallow said, remembering how he and his brothers had rescued their father Danny from that strange country long ago. 'Where will the wolves run away to? Where will the stoats and weasels and the pinemartins go to escape, and the badgers and hedgehogs and shrews and mice and rats, and the rabbits and squirrels? Which way will they run?'

'Not this way,' said Danny. 'They'll go with the wind away from the fire which follows the wind – the way those clouds of smoke are blowing.'

'A pity,' said Swallow, who was hungry as usual.

The birds were crying high above them in a sky where they only had seen crows, larks and once or twice a golden eagle until now. The birds were circling and calling to each other.

'They have lost their nests,' said Danny. Then suddenly he and Swallow heard a growly fierce voice very close to them.

'I've lost my nest,' it said.

They looked about them.

'I see nothing,' Swallow said.

'Foxes know nothing,' the strange voice said, and now it sounded like a cat's but deeper.

Danny Fox and Swallow sniffed about them, hoping to smell the animal that spoke. They could not see it, and at first they could not smell it because of the acrid smoke that spoiled the mountain air. Then a strong scent reached Swallow's nostrils.

'It's a cat,' he said to Danny. 'But not an ordinary cat.'

Then they saw the heather moving. And then they saw a cat step out of it towards them, a tabby cat almost twice the size of the farmer's cat, but thin and weak. Her eyes were dim, her coat was burnt in patches, her step uncertain. She faltered, wavering from side to side as she walked between the clumps of heather on to the smooth mountain path. And now both Danny's and Swallow's hair stood on end.

'Who are you?' said Danny in a fierce voice. He did not like to see strangers near his den.

The cat sat down beside him. 'I am Shaggy the Wild Cat,' she said. 'I am tired and hungry.'

'If you're hungry,' said Danny, 'go down to the bottom of the mountain to the farmer's house and say miaow and they'll bring you a saucer of milk.'

'Cats have an easy life,' said Swallow. 'People like them.'

Shaggy stood up proudly and showed her claws. 'I am a Wild Cat, I tell you. I get nothing from people. But I am old and toothless and my sight is dim. I cannot hunt. That is why I am hungry.'

'Cats are cats,' said Swallow, 'wild or tame. The farmer will feed stray cats, but not stray foxes.'

'The farmer is a man,' said Shaggy the Wild Cat. 'Men are my enemies.'

'The farmer is our enemy,' said Swallow and Danny Fox together.

'His cat is your enemy too,' said Shaggy the Wild Cat.

'What?'

'He has a tame cat called Lady Shiny.'

Danny Fox looked at Shaggy with his head on one side as he always looked when something puzzled him. 'How can you know that?' he said. 'You come from the strange forest country.'

'Count the black rings on my tail,' said Shaggy the Wild Cat, stiffly.

Danny counted seven.

'Seven. A magical number. But if you count the black tip and the fur at the top that once was black and is now a grey smudge because I am old, you can count nine. Seven and nine are magical numbers. And a ring is a magical shape.'

Neither Danny Fox nor Swallow could understand what she meant. They stared at her half afraid, half wishing to help her.

'Magical? What's that?' said Danny. And Swallow said, 'Why did you come this way if you didn't want to find the farmer? Why didn't you run the way the wind blows with the other animals?'

'I go my own way,' said Shaggy quietly.

'And what do you want?'

'To find a tree.'

'What for?' said Danny Fox who hated trees because long ago, the wolves had trapped him in the forest.

'My nest was in a hollow tree,' said Shaggy, 'and now it is burnt down I must find another.'

'There is not one single tree on our mountain,' Danny Fox said.

Shaggy the Wild Cat stalked off in her secret way, making no sound, and Danny went down the path smelling the air and watching for any movement that meant danger. The world that day seemed filled with dangers because the smell of burning hid the ordinary smells that he was used to. Swallow ran off at a gallop, bounding through the heather.

Then Mrs Doxie Fox came out of the den and ran after her husband Danny; 'What a horrible, smoky smell,' she said. 'But the baby's asleep. Let's go and search for food.'

The baby was asleep when Mrs Doxie Fox left the den. But soon the smell of burning woke her and she found herself alone. It was dark. She was not afraid of the dark but she was afraid of being alone. It had always been dark in the cave where she lived with her father Danny Fox and her mother Mrs Doxie Fox. The floor of the cave was made of warm earth, and a prickly curtain of hawthorn kept the light out and the wind away. And every time she had woken up before that day, she had felt her mother's furry tummy against her nose and smelt its lovely smell, and felt her mother's long bushy tail about her back like a scarf. Her mother had always been with her, so she thought. And her father was often there too. She did not know that they had to eat, that they had to go out and search for food, and that her mother never went out until her baby was happily asleep. And now the cave smelt nasty. She sneezed.

She felt for her mother and began to walk and sniff about the cave. She heard a sighing sound and cocked her ears towards it. It was the sound of the wind in the leaves of the hanging hawthorn bush that hid the entrance to the cave. She turned her nose towards the sound, trying to smell it, and for the first time she saw. She saw light. She crept out through the mouth of the cave, beneath the hawthorn and on to the bare mountainside.

Now she was very much afraid. 'There is no one in this wide place,' she thought, and yelped.

Then suddenly she saw a large shadow. There was something behind her. She began to run. She heard the pebbles scrabble, and sharp claws dug into her hind leg, making her squeal with pain.

She ran and she ran and the creature was bounding after her. She came to a wide flat rock which was split down the middle by a crack just wide enough to let her through. She dived into the darkness of this cleft in the rock expecting to land on an earthy floor where she could hide.

But for a long time there was no floor. And tumbledy, tumbledy down in the dark she fell, bumpedy bumpedy on the stone wall of the crack, until – squelch – she could fall no further. Splidgy, splodgy, spludge, she floundered in cold mud at the bottom. It was soft. She was not hurt. She liked the darkness and began to clean herself, licking the mud off her fur, and the spots of blood from her leg.

It was Shaggy the Wild Cat who had stalked the baby fox, while the sun cast her shadow before her. But she could not see very well and when she sprang she only scratched the baby's leg, and of course she was too big to get down the crack. She stood quite still, looking down into the darkness and trying to smell what was there. When the baby fox grew hungry she began to cry. She howled and howled as she longed for her mother and her howls were so unhappy and loud that they rose through the cleft and rang on the rocks above and echoed on the mountain cliffs outside, until they reached the ears of her elder brother Swallow, who was nosing about for berries among some stunted bushes that grew near the mountain top. Swallow looked up and cocked his ears. As soon as he recognized his baby sister's voice he ran helter-skelter down the mountain until he came to the cleft in the flat rock. And there was Shaggy the Wild Cat standing over it, peering down.

'What are you doing here?' said Swallow.

'I was chasing a rat. It ran into that crack.'

'A rat?' said Swallow, looking down into the crack where he saw nothing but darkness. He could hear something scrabbling in the mud far below. He barked and the baby answered. He snapped at Shaggy, 'That's not a rat. It's my baby sister.' Shaggy arched her back at him, then moved a little way off.

'Can't you climb up?' Swallow called to the baby.

'No,' said the baby, 'or I wouldn't stay down here, would I? All wet and cold and hungry. And a sore leg.'

'Wait a minute then,' said Swallow, 'and when you see my tail hanging down the crack, catch hold of it with your teeth and I'll pull you up.'

Swallow was a kind and helpful fox, but not very clever. When he found that his tail was too short, he said, 'Wait a minute till I fetch my brother Chew. He's got a longer tail.'

'I can't help waiting, can I?' said the baby.

Chew came, but his tail was only an inch longer than Swallow's and it dangled far above the baby's head. 'Wait a minute,' said Swallow, 'I've got an idea. I'll fetch our eldest brother Lick. He's got the longest tail of all.'

But Lick's tail was only half an inch longer than Chew's and it too dangled far above the baby's head.

'We'll have to think of another plan,' said Lick.

'Let's run to the beach and borrow the fisherman's rope,' said Chew.

'Too far,' said Swallow.

Just at that moment their parents arrived, having followed their scent on the mountain paths and heard the commotion.

'What are you all doing there?' said Danny Fox, the father of them all. He swished his tail. He looked fierce and brave in his thick red coat.

'Come quickly,' said their mother, Mrs Doxie Fox, so long and slim and sleek. 'The baby's lost. Come. Search the hills.'

'We've found the baby,' Swallow said. 'That's why we are here.'

They explained what had happened and offered to run to the fisherman's house for the rope. But Mrs Doxie Fox was almost in despair. She called to her baby and though she could not see her she could hear how far away she was at the bottom of the deep, dark crack. 'The baby couldn't hold on to a rope,' she said. 'Her mouth is small. Her teeth are tiny. She is too young.'

'That is true,' said Danny.

'Oh how can we save her?'

'By sticks and stones,' said Danny, and immediately he sent Lick, Chew and Swallow out on to the mountain to fetch twigs of heather, sticks from bushes, and pebbles as large as they could carry in their mouths. He called down to the baby, telling her not to be afraid when sticks and stones came tumbling down but to shelter in a corner when she heard them falling and climb on top of the pile as it grew.

'We'll soon be back,' Mrs Doxie Fox called out and ran after Danny to fetch sticks and stones.

Now there was a pitter-patter, patter-pitter on the mountain path as the five foxes passed each other again and again, running up with their mouths closed and down with their white teeth showing against the dark objects they carried. Danny saw Swallow's wide-open mouth with a thick bushy twig of heather clenched between strong teeth. When Doxie saw Chew with a big black pebble between his gaping jaws, she said, 'Be careful! Don't break your teeth!' But Chew ran on as though he did not hear her. Both Danny and Doxie met Lick with the largest load of all between his splendid teeth and gathering what they could find they raced back to the cleft in the rock. They dropped the sticks and stones down the dark crack where the baby had fallen. When Swallow's bushy piece of heather got stuck half way, Chew dropped his big black pebble on to it and sent it down. When Danny's clump of grassy roots got stuck, Lick dropped a heavy stone on to it and sent it down. And gradually, as all the five foxes ran to and fro to fetch more things, the little baby climbed the growing pile. She sheltered in a corner every time the sticks and stones came crashing down, then climbed on top of them, until at last the pile rose high enough for her to crawl out to her mother. Her mother licked her, then picked her up by the scruff of the neck and gripping her gently with her teeth, carried her homewards. Danny Fox and his grown-up sons, Lick, Chew and Swallow, followed her down the path in single file.

Outside the den the baby began to whine again with hunger and her mother put her down and let her suck. Danny Fox and the young foxes were watching. They thought it funny to see the baby drink so fast. Danny Fox wagged his tail and said 'She'll choke!' Mrs Doxie Fox looked up at him while her baby was still sucking and said, 'Now you've named her! We couldn't think of a name.'

'How have I named her?' said Danny.

'We named our eldest children Lick, Chew and Swallow, because they were always so hungry and greedy. And now the name of our hungry baby is Choke.'

The baby was full of milk by now and began to hiccup, and as her mother washed her, licking the scratches that Shaggy had made, licking the mud off everywhere, turning her over and holding her down with a paw, she hiccupped more than ever.

When it was over she sat up and saw Swallow. She growled. Her hair stood on end and she backed away.

'That's your brother, who found you. Don't be afraid,' said her mother, Mrs Doxie Fox.

'Then why does he not live at home with us in the den?' said Choke.

'He is grown up. He likes to live by himself.'

Then Choke saw Lick, a great big fox, and she growled fiercely.

'That is another brother who helped to rescue you.'

'Then why does he not live at home in the den?'

'He lives at the top of the mountain with his wife.'

'I'm going home to her now,' said Lick and he ran away.

'His fur is dark red, like mine,' said Danny, 'but his wife's fur is pale. She looks white in the moonlight.'

When Choke saw Chew, another strange fox, she bared her little teeth and snarled, but they told her not to be afraid, for Chew like the others was a grown-up brother who would always help her and look after her.

'Then why does he not live at home in the den?' said Choke.

'He lives with his wife by the sea.'

'I'm going home to her now,' said Chew and ran away.

'His fur is paler than mine,' said Danny, 'but his wife is dark, almost black, and on a moonless night you can't see her.'

The baby fox heard stealthy footsteps in the heather 'Is this the dark fox coming?' she said.

It was not the dark fox. It was Shaggy the Wild Cat who had been watching them all this time and following them at a distance. She peered and sniffed at the baby. The baby hid beneath her mother's tummy.

'That's not a rat,' said Shaggy.

'I told you it's my baby sister,' Swallow said. 'You scratched her.'

Shaggy the Wild Cat did not say she was sorry. She walked a little way off and sat down.

'You are lame,' said Swallow.

She was too proud to answer. She licked the pads of all her four paws in turn as though there was no one in the world who cared about her. The pads of her paws had burns on them, because when she left her nest in the burning tree she ran over the floor of the forest, which looked grey with ashes but had red-hot pine needles underneath.

'If you want to make a new nest,' said Danny, 'there's a big wood near the Palace on the far side of the town.'

'People!' said Shaggy the Wild Cat in a nasty voice, and went on licking her paws.

Then Swallow said, 'You can stay with me if you like. My den is in the loneliest part of the mountain. It's large and dark. And I'm alone.'

'What can there be to eat up there?' said Shaggy the Wild Cat, gazing towards the craggy heights.

'Oh, I'll find something,' said Swallow.

'I'm going down to the fisherman's house,' said Danny Fox, 'to see if he can spare us some fish. If he gives me any, we'll save one for you.'

Swallow and Shaggy the Wild Cat walked off together up the mountain path, and Danny ran down towards the seashore where the fisherman's house was.

'We must go to our cave and sleep,' said Mrs Doxie Fox to Choke. She took hold of the baby's furry neck in her teeth and carried her under the hawthorn curtain, and they lay down together and slept in the dark.

2. Danny Scares the Queen

The fisherman and his wife were the only people in the world who were kind to Danny Fox. They lived in a small, lonely house so close to the sea that at high tide in stormy weather the waves would break against the window and the front door. The back door opened on to the stony path that came down the mountain from the foxes' cave. It had a hole in it near the ground to allow the fisherman's dog to come in and out as he pleased.

When Danny Fox came scampering down the steep path, scattering pebbles in his hurry, he suddenly heard an angry voice coming from inside the house. Danny stopped to listen. Then he crept up to the back door and peeped through the hole.

The fisherman and his wife were standing with their backs to the fire. Both had bare feet and their clothes were worn and ragged. The fisherman's trousers had so many patches that you could not tell what colour they had been when they were new. He had been tarring his nets and his shirt was smudged with tar. He had torn it on a nail and its sleeves were frayed like the leaves of a fern. His black curly hair was tangled by the wind and sticky with sea spray.

He was young and handsome and hard and thin, and his face and hands were stained with tar like his shirt because he had just come in from work. 'He is the best man in the world,' thought Danny.

The fisherman's wife was a princess, but no one would have thought it, to look at her now. Her beautiful face was tarry too because she had been helping with the nets, and her yellow hair hung down about her shoulders unbrushed and salty from spray, straggling like seaweed. She was wearing her husband's old blue jersey with holes at the elbows and a faded red skirt with blue patches on it. Her legs were bare and dusty from the ashes of the fire. 'She is the best woman in the world,' thought Danny.

Her stepmother, the Queen, was standing in the middle of the room in her second-best shoes which were made of cloth of gold with high silver heels, and her second-best robe which was made of damask, a rich kind of silk with patterns woven into it, her second-best crown on her head, pure gold but without jewels, and in her hand a long ebony walking stick with a gold knob at the top. She was waving the walking stick angrily at the Princess and the fisherman and shouting at them in an ugly voice that Danny remembered hearing long ago. 'She is the worst woman in the world,' thought Danny Fox.

'Come home with me to the palace!' shrieked the Queen.

'This is my home,' the Princess said. 'I like it better,

and besides I'm never going to leave my husband. Never!'

'Your husband is a disgrace.'

'You liked me before we got married,' the fisherman said. 'You arranged our wedding, your Majesty. It was a beautiful wedding, thank you very much.'

'I was tricked into letting you marry!' The Queen was shouting and waving her stick. 'I was tricked by that nasty Danny Fox. You know how he made you dress up in fine clothes, to make me think you were rich.'

'It was my best trick,' said Danny Fox proudly, creeping a little further into the room. None of them heard or saw him. His hindquarters were still outside and his tail was wagging as he remembered how he had filled many sacks with dry leaves and pretended to the Queen that they were full of five pound notes belonging to the fisherman.

'My husband is still the same man,' the Princess said, 'rich or poor. Grand clothes won't make me love him more.'

'Then why doesn't he offer me a chair. To keep the Queen standing in the middle of the kitchen floor! He's a disgrace.'

'I did, your Majesty,' the fisherman said, picking up the one chair he had and placing it beside her. 'You said you'd rather stand.'

'There was a spider on it, and a black slug on the leg. Show me into the drawing-room.'

'We haven't got a drawing-room,' the Princess said.

'Into your bedroom then. I must speak to you alone.'

'This is our bedroom and our kitchen and everything. There's only one room in the house and I love it,' said the Princess.

'Then where does that door lead to?' said the Queen pointing to the back door with her stick. Danny Fox crouched down and drew back.

'It leads to the mountain,' the Princess said.

'A back door and a front door in one room!' screamed the Queen. 'I've never heard of such a thing!' The fisherman explained, 'When the wind blows from the sea, we open the back door. When the wind blows from the mountain we open the front door.'

'It is a disgrace. I am taking the Princess home with me at once. She can't live here a moment longer!'

'You know I won't go,' said the Princess quietly.

'You won't go?' The Queen's face was red with anger. She was standing with her feet wide apart and Danny thought she would hit the Princess with the gold knob of her stick. The high silver heels of her shoes were showing beneath her long robe. Danny came crouching into the room behind her and lifted the hem of her robe with his nose. Inside he found a petticoat, then another and another and another – six altogether. He lifted each one gently with his nose and crawled underneath and sat between her legs.

'Then,' said the Queen, 'your husband can come too. My Grand Master of the Bath will give him a wash and I'll find him a nice job with good money. He will start as my High Mixer of Dainty Cakes.'

The Princess burst out laughing and the Queen raised her stick to beat her, but when Danny felt her move he touched her leg with his long whiskers.

The stick clattered down on to the stone floor and she screamed.

'The spider!' said the Queen in a hoarse frightened whisper. 'Oh take it away. It's crawling on my leg. I'll stand quite still.'

The Princess stepped forward to look under her skirt. Danny Fox, not wanting her to see him, kept his whiskers away from the Queen's leg.

'It's gone now,' said the Queen. 'Give me my stick.' When the Princess gave it to her she pointed it at the fisherman. 'I command you to be my Mixer of Dainty Cakes,' she said.

'I can't mix cakes, your Majesty. I am a fisherman.'

'You can't? How dare you disobey the Queen?' She waved her stick at him but in a moment she was screaming with fear because Danny Fox had put his shiny black wet nose against her ankle.

'It's that slug,' said the Queen. 'It's on my ankle. Oh!'

The Princess lifted up the hem of the Queen's robe and the hems of all the six petticoats and looked straight into Danny's shining eyes. 'You!' she gasped. 'You naughty thing. How did you get in there?'

'It's no use speaking to a slug, you silly girl. Just pick it up and throw it out.'

Danny began to come out through the gap the Princess had made, but she pushed him in again and whispered. 'Go out at the back and run. You mustn't be seen. It will go in a minute,' she said to the Queen.

'Dust and spiders and slugs!' said the Queen. 'What a dreadful place for a Princess to live in! I'm going home. My carriage is outside. You get into it first.'

'I'm not going, your Majesty. Please don't be cross with me.'

'If you are not outside the door in five seconds, I shall send my soldiers to fetch you. One. Two. Three. Four . . .'

But instead of saying five, she gave a loud shriek and waved her arms because Danny nipped the calf of her leg with his little front teeth. It did not hurt her much, but tore her second-best silk stocking and gave her such a fright that she jumped in the air lifting Danny Fox with her, tangled in her petticoats. Danny wriggled and squirmed and tried to burrow his way out with his nose and all four feet, and all the folds of silk and satin wound themselves about him till his tail and hind legs became twisted round one of the Queen's legs and his head and forelegs round the other. The Queen fell. Her screams turned

into a wailing moan. The fisherman was just in time to save her from banging her head on the stone floor. She fainted away in his arms.

'That's funny,' he said to the Princess. 'The top part has fainted; her arms are quite limp. But her legs are kicking away like mad beneath her robes.'

A second later, he almost dropped the Queen because he saw her under-petticoat, the sixth one, which was blue and dotted with gold stars and crescent moons, come out from under her robe of its own accord. It wriggled about the room like a long snake with a big head, as though it had lost its way, until it reached the back door. Then its head shot out through the hole trailing the long starry tail behind it. The fisherman turned pale.

'Don't you faint too,' the Princess said. 'It's only Danny Fox. I'll fetch some water.'

She ran out to the well and was just in time to see the Queen's petticoat wriggling its way up the mountain path.

'Danny Fox! Danny Fox!' the Princess called as she lowered her bucket into the well. 'Leave the petticoat behind. I'll give it back to her.'

'I can't,' said Danny's muffled voice. 'I can't get out.'

'Please try.'

'All right,' said Danny, 'but she's got five others.' He sat down inside the petticoat holding it firmly with his paws and bit a hole in it. He pushed his head through, but could not get any further. The Princess pulled up her bucket of water and saw what he had done.

'Oh you've torn it!' she said.

'I can see better now,' said Danny.

'Go quickly and hide, and bring it back tonight and I'll mend it. Oh you are naughty,' the Princess said as she went back to the house.

'Naughty?' said Danny. 'I saved you from the soldiers, didn't I?'

'I hope so,' the Princess said. 'I'm not sure yet.'

She and the fisherman revived the Queen with a cupful of cold water and carried her out to her carriage and asked the coachman to drive her home to the palace.

3. The Starry Petticoat

In the evening, as the sun was going down, Mrs Doxie Fox brought her baby out to play. The baby pushed round pebbles with her nose, then pounced on them when they started rolling down the hill, and she picked up dead twigs of heather and worried and shook them and tossed them away, but the game she liked best was pretending to fight with her mother. Mrs Doxie Fox would lie on her back with floppy paws and Choke would climb on to her chest and bite her throat, but her mouth was so small that she could only tug the fur. Then her mother would shake her off and catch her by the throat with her big teeth, pretending to be fierce, and when she let her free again Choke would pounce on her mother's open mouth and seize the lower jaw in hers and bite as hard as she could. Sometimes she hurt her mother's tongue with her sharp little teeth and her mother would roll her over and stand above her holding her down with one paw and biting her nose with gentle pretending bites. And all the time they would growl at each other in a playful tone.

Their game was interrupted that evening by a weird swishing sound that frightened Mrs Doxie Fox.

She let go of Choke and her growl became quite different – deep and fierce. She looked down the mountain path and saw a long, blue twisty creature crawling up towards them. It looked like a dragon or a snake, but as it came closer she saw that its skin was dotted with stars and crescent moons. 'Look out,' she said to the baby. 'A bit of the sky has fallen down – a bit of the night sky.'

'Will it swallow us up?' asked Choke, and that reminded Mrs Doxie Fox that Swallow was probably not far away. She pointed her nose to the ground and howled for him. Then she barked at the strange crawling thing. Her voice was heard all over the mountain and the echoing rocks gave an answer.

Danny Fox was crawling home because the many folds of the Queen's petticoat were entangled in his feet. He could not run or even walk properly and, although his head was sticking out through the hole he had bitten, he was holding it low near the ground to prevent Mrs Doxie Fox from seeing it. He had decided, as usual, to play a trick on her.

If she and the baby had been able to smell him they would have recognized him from far away, but his own scent was smothered by a very strong scent of bath-salts, soap and talcum-powder, which seemed to them strange and alarming. The Queen had nine baths every day and, just before she had left to visit the Princess and the fisherman, she had ordered her Grand Master of the Bath to prepare a very thick

bath that looked and felt like pea-soup and smelt of
mint. The soap was made of mint, cloves, musk,
ambergris, camphor, frangipane, which is the flower
of the red jasmine, and bergamot, the juice of the
Prince's Pear. And the talcum was made of powdered
sandal wood and orris root. She knew all these scents
would cling to her after her bath and keep away the
smell of fish she expected to find in the fisherman's
house, and of course the strong mixture clung to her
petticoat too.

'Who are you? What are you?' said Mrs Doxie
Fox, backing away with her baby behind her.

'I am the Queen,' said Danny in a funny voice.
Mrs Doxie Fox believed him. She had often tried to
imagine what the Queen looked like. She knew she
was some kind of dragon.

'Oh then you won't hurt us, will you?' she said.
'You know my husband Danny Fox.'

'Call me your Majesty,' said Danny.

'Yes, your Majesty. Danny Fox, your Majesty, is
a friend, your Majesty, of your Majesty's Princess,
your Majesty.'

'That's why I have come to see you,' said Danny. 'Prince Danny Fox is now at the palace, curled up asleep on the throne. The Grand Master of the Bath is getting his bath ready and the High Mixer of Dainty Bones, Cheese and Porridge is mixing him the biggest meal he has ever had in his life and all because he was so very kind to me this afternoon.'

'What did he do?' said Mrs Doxie Fox, afraid that he might have played a trick on the Queen which only seemed to be kind.

'My petticoat was hurting me. It's made of scratchy stuff. He took it away.'

'Oh dear,' said Mrs Doxie Fox who thought a petticoat must be something to eat. 'I hope it doesn't choke him if it's scratchy.'

'I'm here,' said Choke, when she heard her name. While they were talking, she had crept forward and begun to play with the petticoat, taking it in her teeth and trying to tear it. Danny Fox felt an itch in his ear and tried to scratch it but his hind leg was held fast by the petticoat and he tumbled over, bringing the baby with him. She rolled on to his head and as soon as she smelt his real scent she knew who it was and began to lick his face.

'Don't lick the Queen's face,' said Mrs Doxie Fox.

'The Queen would be much obliged if you bit her left ear which is somewhat itchy. The Queen has one or two fleas,' said Danny in a grand voice.

Just then, Swallow came galloping down the

mountain. He had heard his mother calling and soon he stood beside them, panting, his pink tongue hanging out between white teeth. Shaggy the Wild Cat was limping along behind him, tired and slow.

'What a funny smell,' said Swallow.

'It is the Queen,' said Mrs Doxie Fox. 'You must say "What a funny smell *your Majesty*."'

'What a funny queen, your Majesty,' said Swallow.

'Her Majesty has very kindly taken Danny to the Palace to give him a bath.'

'Well I hope he doesn't come home with all the nasty scent on him,' said Swallow.

'It is delicious,' said Shaggy. 'I can smell catmint. And this starry thing looks nice and soft to lie on.'

She stepped on to the petticoat and felt about for the softest place. 'It is beautifully padded,' she said, lying down on Danny's bushy tail. 'It's stuffed with fur, I think.'

'I wish you would send Danny home, your Majesty,' said Mrs Doxie Fox.

It was Swallow who answered her. He said, 'Perhaps my father Danny Fox is at the Palace sitting on the throne with the Queen's head on his neck. And here's the poor Queen crawling along with Danny's head. And an itch in one ear. Queens can't scratch their ears with their hind feet you know.'

Swallow came closer and sniffed Danny's face. 'It's Danny's head, all right,' he said. 'Whatever can have happened to the rest of him?'

Danny Fox knew he had been found out and besides he was tired of this game, but what with the weight of the cat on his tail and the tangle of cloth about his legs, which had grown tighter when he tried to scratch, he could not stand up. He asked Swallow to help him to take the petticoat off. But neither Swallow nor Mrs Doxie Fox had ever seen a petticoat before. They did not even look for the open ends. They thought it was shaped like a sack and tried to pull Danny through the hole he had bitten.

'Don't tear it any more,' said Danny. 'I promised the Princess.'

'But how on earth did you get into it?'

'I don't know. I was hiding in a tent, and suddenly the tent-poles gave way and all this fell on top of me.'

'I'll make four little holes for your feet,' said Swallow. 'Then you can walk more easily.' But Danny would not allow him to do that. He knew the Princess would understand how to get out of a petticoat. He saw that the sun had gone down behind the mountain. It was almost dark. The Queen would be at home in her palace by now. He could safely go back to the fisherman's house.

'Get up, Shaggy,' he said. 'You are lying on my tail.' But Shaggy was sound asleep.

Swallow nudged her with his nose. He had grown rather fond of her, and had found her things to eat that day because she could not see well enough to hunt. He woke her up.

'May I have this thing,' she said. 'I have no warm nest to sleep in nowadays.'

'I'm sorry,' said Danny Fox. 'I promised to take it back.'

Shaggy stepped sleepily off the petticoat and said, 'Good-bye' to them all.

When Danny Fox was sure he was too far away for them to hear him, he began to whine as he stumbled down the mountain with the heavy petticoat cramping his legs. Even his tail was twisted by the rich folding cloth and he felt uneasy. He wondered how he could escape if the farmer saw him or what he could do if he met another danger – the wolf who lived in the forest. Even when there was no danger he liked to run fast. The petticoat made him feel that he was not Danny Fox any more, that he had lost his strength and lost his tricks as well.

Of course he could have torn it to pieces and got out of it, but he did not want to give the Princess too much mending, so he laboured his way down the mountain and arrived, whimpering, at her back door. He looked in through the hole which belonged to the old dog and the dog looked at him growling. But the Princess heard his sad, whining voice and pulled him in. She was alone. The fisherman was out in his boat.

'My tricks have all gone away,' said Danny Fox. 'This starry petticoat has weakened me.'

'I'll take it off. But I can't believe your tricks have gone.'

Danny Fox lay down on the stone floor and she began to disentangle the Queen's sixth petticoat from his tail and legs and neck.

'Now pull in your head,' she said, 'and I'll let you out if you walk backwards.'

But as he was walking backwards, they heard a sound like twelve big hammers hammering the pebbles of the beach. Six soldiers marched into the room stamping their twelve feet. They thumped the stone floor with the butts of their guns and the first one shouted, 'We arrest you in the name of Her Majesty the Queen.'

Danny did not care how much he tore the petticoat now. He held it down with his paws and ripped it open with his teeth and sprang out. He leapt at the first soldier's legs and tripped him up. The old dog, who had been barking all the time, came to help him and together they knocked the second soldier down, but the others hit them with their guns and they had

to take refuge under the bed. When they saw the first two soldiers seize the Princess and put chains on her ankles and wrists, they rushed out again and tried to bite their legs, but their teeth slipped on the shiny leather boots. They could not save the Princess. The soldiers carried her out of the house and up the beach to the road and locked her into a black carriage with barred windows. They drove her away towards the town, towards the palace she hated so much.

4. Danny Slips into the Palace

'What shall we do?' the old dog said. 'My master won't be home from the sea till morning.'

'He couldn't rescue her,' said Danny Fox. 'And nor can we, just now. I am going away to think. Tell him I shall be back as soon as I've thought of a trick. I'm taking this horrid thing with me.' He gave the petticoat a savage bite and ripped another hole in it. Then he dragged it up the mountain after him. The old dog stayed to guard the house. He felt lonely for his mistress, the Princess, and sat on the beach outside the front door whining sadly. He watched the sea all night for the lights of the fisherman's boat. Sometimes he howled at the moon and sometimes he barked gruffly at the moving shadow of a cloud.

Danny Fox left the petticoat outside his den and went in. Choke was asleep, but he saw Mrs Doxie Fox's eyes gleaming in the darkness.

'The Princess has been stolen and carried away in chains,' said Danny Fox. 'How can I save her?'

'By one of your tricks,' said Mrs Doxie Fox.

Danny sat down. He did not even scratch himself or chase his tail, which he usually did when he came home. He just sat staring at her. She licked his face.

'Why are you sad?' she said.

'Because I have no tricks left. The Queen and her horrid petticoat have taken them away.'

'Lie down,' said Mrs Doxie Fox. 'A trick will come into your head while you're asleep.'

But Danny stood up and shook himself and said, 'I'm going out.' When he was at the opening of the cave, he came back to her and gave her a little bite on the neck in the way she bit her baby. She tried to bite him back but he was gone.

Danny Fox seized the tattered petticoat in his teeth and galloped up the mountain to Swallow's den. He saw Swallow dragging something larger than himself across the rocks and called to him. Swallow lived in the loneliest part of the mountain where the rock was bare. No bushes or heather grew there, only some tiny rock flowers and thin patches of hard, spiky grass.

'How did you get that big cheese?' said Danny Fox.

'The farmer's wife threw it out.'

'A big cheese like that! She threw it out?'

'She sometimes does,' said Swallow, 'when she's making lots of cheeses and one goes wrong. She meant it for the pigs.'

Danny Fox looked at it hungrily. It was as big as the wheel of a wheelbarrow.

'The pigs get plenty to eat,' said Swallow. 'They are fat. Shaggy the Wild Cat has had nothing for days.'

'It's a good thing you found it,' said Danny, 'because I got no fish at the fisherman's house. There was no time to think about fish.'

Danny Fox told Swallow what had happened.

'The present is not for me,' said Swallow. 'It's for Shaggy the Wild Cat. She is old and has lost her teeth. I had to find something soft like cheese for her to eat.'

Danny, keeping hold of the petticoat, managed to take one side of the large round cheese in his teeth as well and together they dragged it to the top of the steep rock above Swallow's den.

'Let's rest,' said Swallow, and they sat down. 'Shaggy's a bit of a nuisance,' he said. 'She won't eat fruit, and can't see enough to catch even a beetle. That's why she's so thin.'

'Perhaps she won't stay long,' said Danny.

'Oh, she can if she wants to. My den is large and lonely.'

With the cheese and the starry petticoat they scrambled down the slope and stood outside the entrance to Swallow's den, which was under a ledge of rock so low that you had to crawl to get in or out.

'Hullo,' said Shaggy, peering out from the darkness. 'It is cold in here and the floor is hard.'

'I've brought you a warm bed,' said Danny Fox, 'with the moon and stars on it.'

'And I've brought you your supper,' Swallow said.

Shaggy crawled out. It was lighter outside, for

there was a moon behind some clouds, but she looked like a shadow. She smelt the cheese cautiously – for though she was hungry she would not eat in a hurry. Then she tore small pieces from it and chewed them with her gums and the few teeth she had left. Danny Fox and Swallow helped themselves too.

When they had finished Danny Fox said, 'The Princess has been stolen and carried away in chains. How can we save her?'

Shaggy the Wild Cat did not even answer. She sat down and washed her face carefully as though that was the only thing that mattered, slowly licking each paw and wiping her cheeks and mouth with each in turn. Then she stood up and stretched herself, then stood quite still gazing into the distance. She could see better at night than in the day.

At that moment the wind blew the clouds away from the moon and Danny Fox and Swallow saw her clearly in the pale moonlight, a gaunt and secret creature like no cat they had ever seen before. Her broad thick tail stretched out behind her in a straight line with her back. The seven black rings on it looked like bracelets, and along her straight back there was

a line of dark fur with stripes leading from it down her flanks till they mingled and disappeared into the grey and fawn and sandy gold hairs of the rest of her body. A lot of her fur had fallen out. She had been ill and half starved and burned. But she still looked fierce and beautiful. Her face was like a tiger's, marked with curving black lines. As they watched her she shuddered. Her whole body shuddered and shook, and without one glance at the foxes she crouched, and crawled into the cave. Danny and Swallow dragged the cheese in after her and Danny went out to fetch the petticoat as well.

Shaggy the Wild Cat smelled every part of the petticoat carefully, then sat down on the softest part.

'Are you very old?' asked Danny Fox.

'Very old,' she said.

'Are you very wise?'

'Very wise.'

'Then tell us how to save the Princess.'

'By magic,' said Shaggy the Wild Cat with a disdainful glance at him.

'Is that a kind of trick?'

'It's stronger than a trick. It can be bad and it can be good. Magic will keep the Princess in prison. Magic could set her free.'

'Then teach me good magic,' said Danny, but she only answered, 'All foxes know some tricks. All cats know some magic. And I know more magic than any other cat in the world.'

'But how can we rescue her?' said Danny again.

'You must go to the palace and find out where the prison is,' said Shaggy. 'And then you must find the keys. You can find the prison by looking. You can find the keys by listening.'

'But how?' said Danny Fox.

'Inside a man that is not a man,
You will hear a jingle-jangle that is not a bell.'

She would not explain her riddle. Turning away from Danny Fox she stared at Swallow and her eyes were like two red lamps in the darkness. 'And you, Swallow,' she said, 'while your father is listening and looking you must watch Lady Shiny, the farmer's cat. You must follow her everywhere and come back and tell me where she goes and what she does.'

Shaggy the Wild Cat would say no more. She curled herself up on the Queen's petticoat and fell asleep.

Swallow went down to the farm at once to look for Lady Shiny, and Danny ran all the way to the town. It was still dark, in the very early morning, when he reached the market square.

The Royal Palace was the tallest building in the square. It was so tall that he could not see the upper windows from the pavement. He scratched the front door with his paw and listened for footsteps. He barked a few times and scratched again, but no one came. So he crossed to the opposite side of the square from where he could see the topmost windows, and sat down in the doorway of a little baker's shop to wait until one of the palace lights came on.

Of all the people in the town, the baker was the first to get up. He had to bake bread for everybody's breakfast and cakes for tea and that meant lighting a large wood fire inside his oven at four o'clock every morning. Soon Danny heard him come downstairs. He crouched in the shadows of the doorway, watching the windows of the palace. The second person to get up every morning was the Queen's High Mixer of Dainty Cakes. The Queen did not know it, but he did not mix the dainty cakes at all. He got up every morning before anyone else in the palace was awake and secretly crossed the square to the baker's to fetch a lot of rough-looking ordinary cakes from the oven,

then when he got back to the palace he prodded and smoothed them into dainty shapes and smothered them in different kinds of goo-ey icing which the Queen liked. He lived on the top floor of the palace.

At five o'clock exactly Danny saw him light his candle, and watched him dress in his dainty cake mixer's suit. Through the windows of the palace staircase, he watched him tiptoeing down, with the candle in his hand, to the ground floor. Then Danny leapt from the baker's doorway and rushed across the square. He held his head against the golden door of the palace. The High Mixer of Dainty Cakes unlocked the door as silently as possible, but as soon as he opened it there was a loud clatter, for Danny, in his hurry to get into the palace, bumped against his legs and gave him such a fright that his candle in its candlestick went flying to the floor. The candle

went out. In the dark, the High Mixer of Dainty Cakes thought a burglar had pushed past him, but he dared not call for help in case the Queen found out about the cakes. He ran across the square to the baker's.

Danny Fox ran up the marble staircase of the Palace and along many corridors, sniffing under every door until he came to the grandest one of all which smelt just like the starry petticoat. He knew this must be the bedroom of the King and Queen and he growled so loudly that the Queen woke up and shouted at the King to stop snoring. Danny sat down and tilted his head to one side to listen.

'I wasn't snoring,' said the King.

'Yes you were. You woke me.'

'I have been lying awake all night thinking of my poor daughter the Princess. Oh please let her out of the dungeon, my dear Queen.'

'Not until she puts the golden dress on. A princess must dress like a princess. She must stay in the dungeon as long as she insists on wearing her rags.'

The King knew the Queen would not listen to him. She never did, and it had become a habit with him to do what she said. But still he went on pleading, because he loved his daughter. Danny sat listening as they argued. He soon found out that when the Princess arrived in the palace she had been carried to her bedroom where all the finest clothes were laid out for her to wear and that the Queen had waited downstairs in the Banqueting Hall for over an hour expecting her to come down beautifully dressed and eat a meal of ninety-nine different dishes ending up with dainty cakes. When the Princess refused to change her clothes or eat, the chains were again attached to her ankles and wrists and she was thrown into a deep, damp dungeon, far below the basement of the palace, a cavern without windows where smelly stagnant pools of rainwater had gathered from last winter on the floor.

Danny Fox ran away from the royal bedroom door and down the marble staircase, turning sideways by the front door, down a granite staircase and a sand-

stone one, and a wooden one and an iron one until he reached the lowest floor of the palace, far below the basement.

Here he found no doors or windows, just a short corridor, paved with large flat stones and ending in a grim black wall. Through a crack between the paving stones, he smelt damp air, like the air that rises from a pool of stagnant water, and he felt sure that the dungeon was below. He put his mouth to the crack and barked softly. A faint voice came from below the ground, so deep down and far away that he could not hear the words. He barked again and listened. At last he heard the Princess calling him by name.

'Danny Fox! Danny Fox!'

'I can hardly hear you,' said Danny. 'Where is the door of the dungeon?'

'Outside,' she said more loudly. 'Go out and round to the back of the palace. It's not a real door. It's an iron grating with bars like the top of a drain.'

'I'll be there in two minutes,' said Danny.

He ran up the stairs, but by this time the High Mixer of Dainty Cakes had come back from the baker's and closed the palace door behind him, pretending he had not been out. Danny was locked in. Soon it would be time for everyone in the palace to get up. He knew he would never be able to save the Princess if he was found. He ran through the Large Banqueting Hall, the Lesser Banqueting Hall and the Little Banqueting Hall, searching for an open window through the Sumptuous Drawing-room, the Superb Drawing-room and the Splendid Drawing-room, through the Luxurious Parlour, the Little Parlour and into the Lazy Parlour, but all the ground-floor windows were closed.

'I wish my tricks would come back to me,' thought Danny Fox and jumped on to the laziest of the lazy chairs, where he sank into the lazy cushions and tried to think.

5. Danny Finds the Dungeon

While Danny Fox was lying in the Lazy Parlour among the lazy cushions of the laziest chair, trying to think how to get out of the palace without being seen, he noticed something that looked like a silver snake dangling down the wall beside him. A little moonlight, shining through one of the windows, made it glitter. It had a large frilly tassel at its end and inside the tassel he could see the snake's head, made of silk, with a pink forked tongue sticking out of its mouth. The tassel and head hung over the arm of his chair. He did not like it. He grabbed it in his teeth, shaking it and jerking the long body of the snake, which was really a fine silken rope attached to a bell-pull near the ceiling. Immediately a hundred bells began to jingle-jangle in the palace and a hundred servants jumped out of bed and ran to the Lazy Parlour, nudging each other and whispering 'The Queen, the Queen! Why is she ringing her bell at this hour of the morning?'

When Danny heard so many footsteps running towards him, he burrowed into the cushions of the Queen's laziest chair and hid. The room was ablaze

with a hundred candles – they carried one each – and the tip of his tail was showing.

'Your Majesty! Where is her Majesty? Her chair is empty.'

But the Grand Master of the Bath saw the white tip of Danny's tail sticking up among the cushions, and said, 'She has left her toothbrush here. She can't be far away.'

'Blow out your candles,' said Danny in his funny Queen's voice. 'I am in my nightie and you mustn't see me.'

They all put out their candles, spluttering and puffing in their hurry to obey.

'I thought so,' said the Grand Master of the Bath. 'She brought her toothbrush with her. She was ringing for her bath. I'll take it up for you, your Majesty.' He could still see the tip of Danny's tail in the moonlight. He took hold of it in his fingers.

'Leave my night-cap alone,' said Danny Fox. 'The

King gave it to me for my birthday, with a special white feather at the top.'

'I beg your pardon, your Majesty. Did you ring for your bath?'

'No,' said Danny. 'I rang because I fainted. Open all the windows and run to fetch the doctor everyone of you.'

The hundred servants opened all the windows and ran together across the market square to wake the doctor up.

As soon as they were gone, Danny jumped up from the cushions and through the biggest window, and landed in the garden of the palace. He wandered round the walls of the palace searching for the grating that looked like the top of a drain. He searched and searched and could not find it until at last he came to a dark yew hedge, thick and gloomy, that had been planted near the Royal Kitchen door to hide the dustbins. He crept under the hedge. The dustbins smelt delicious. They were full to the brim with the ninety-nine dishes the Princess had refused to eat the night before, but he had no time to stop – not even for one mouthful. By the dustbins he saw some stone steps, leading down below the ground. He ran down them and found himself on a twisty staircase, that wound like a corkscrew into a damp dark passage underneath the palace. The passage had pools of water in it and was slippery with green slime. At the end he found a rusty iron grating through which

the water was dripping into the dungeon below. The grating was fixed down by two padlocks, one at each side.

Danny Fox barked softly and this time when the Princess answered he heard her clearly, but he could not see her.

'I knew you would come,' she said. 'So I wasn't afraid.'

'Are you hungry?' asked Danny, thinking of fetching a tasty dish from the dustbin.

'Yes. But I won't eat any of the palace food.'

'I'll find something else,' said Danny. 'And then I shall rescue you. But it may take a day or two until I find the keys and steal them.'

'They are hidden inside the black bishop.' she said, but before he could ask where the black bishop lived, they heard the sound of soldiers tramping on the garden path above.

'Go,' said the Princess. 'They are bringing my bread.'

'Your bread?'

'My breakfast. They push it through the bars – a

slice of dry bread. If they catch you on the staircase I'll never be rescued.'

Danny Fox ran up the winding staircase, twisting and darting as fast as a lizard, and hid just in time beneath the dark yew hedge. He heard the soldiers tramping down the stairs and when they reached the bottom he ran down after them a little way to listen. He heard the chief soldier call to the Princess through the iron grating – 'Her Majesty the Queen is waiting for you to dress in your robes and come to breakfast.'

Then Danny heard the Princess say, 'I am not coming!' When he heard the soldier say 'All right. I shall push your slice of bread through the bars,' he ran from the palace across the fields and along the sea road, without looking back, till he came to the fisherman's house. And all the way as he ran he remembered Shaggy the Wild Cat's riddle:

'Inside a man that is not a man,
You will hear a jingle-jangle that is not a bell.'

'Is a black bishop a man that is not a man?' thought Danny Fox to himself.

The fisherman had come home with only five fish after a whole night on the sea, and he was cold, and he was sad because his princess had been taken away.

'I know where she is,' said Danny Fox.

'Have you seen her?'

'I've heard her. She is living at the bottom of a

dark, damp dungeon. You must take her some fish. She is hungry.'

'Hungry? In the palace!' said the fisherman.

Danny Fox told him why she would not eat and at once the fisherman said he would go and mix dainty cakes for the Queen.

'When the Princess knows I am living in the palace, daintily dressed,' he said, 'she'll put on the grand clothes and at least we'll both have enough to eat, and be together.'

'She would not like you to do that,' said Danny Fox, 'and you won't have to try it, because as soon as I find out where the bishop lives, I shall rescue her.'

The fisherman said, 'The Bishop lives in the Bishop's Palace, I suppose.'

'Has he a palace too,' said Danny Fox, 'with dungeons?'

'It is called a palace,' said the fisherman. 'But it has no dungeons. The bishop is a kind man.'

'I mean the black bishop,' said Danny.

'His coat and breeches are black,' the fisherman said, 'but his gaiters are purple.'

Danny Fox shook himself and sat down to scratch his ear. Then he looked up and said, 'Does his tummy go jingle-jangle as he walks about?'

'Why should it?' asked the fisherman.

'Because he has swallowed the keys of the dungeon. Why are you laughing?' said Danny. He did not like to be laughed at. 'It's true. The Princess told me.'

'Told you what?'

'She said the keys of her dungeon were inside the black bishop. I'm going to get them out. You'll see.'

'And how are you going to do that?'

'I'm going to get a magnet on a string and put it inside a dainty cake, wait till he swallows it. Then pull.'

As he listened to Danny and laughed at him, the fisherman had been cooking a meal for the Princess –

two of the fish and two potatoes which he roasted in their skins on the embers of the fire. When these were ready he wrapped them in a cloth to keep them warm and Danny and he set off along the road to the town. He brought the other three fish with him hoping to sell them in the market place. Danny trotted cautiously a little way ahead, watching for danger, his bushy tail stretched out behind him and his long smooth nose stretched out in front. He growled when he saw the footprints of the soldiers in the dust and the ruts made by the big wheels of the black carriage that had taken the Princess away.

The road to the town went by the seashore for nearly a mile. There was no wall between it and the beach and in bad weather when the tide was high the waves would break across it making it impossible for people to pass, but very few people used it. Only the fisherman went that way every day, and on bad days even fought his way through the breakers, because he was poor and had to sell his fish while they were fresh. The farmer used it once a week, if the weather was good, to buy and sell in the market.

It was market day today – Friday. Near the corner where the road turned inland, away from the sea, towards the town, Danny heard the sound of a pony trotting behind them, a jingle of harness, a creaking of springs and the swish and bumps of fast wheels with iron tyres approaching on the stony, dusty road. He knew it was the farmer's market cart and without looking back jumped quickly over the wall that divided the fields from the road. He hid behind it and lay on the grass to listen.

The farmer pulled up when he reached the fisherman and this is what Danny heard him say.

'Have you seen my cat? She's lost.'

'I haven't seen her,' said the fisherman.

'Why are you walking? Where's your fish cart?'

'I only caught a handful last night. Not worth bringing out the horse.'

'Jump up,' said the farmer. 'I'll give you a lift.'

When Danny heard that he began to run by a short-cut across the fields, hoping to reach the town before them, but he had only gone a little way when he saw Lady Shiny, the farmer's cat, in front of him taking the same short-cut, but slowly, shaking her paws every few steps because she did not like the cool wet drops of the morning dew on the grass. Lady Shiny's fur was perfectly white and her skin pink. Her nose, the pads of her neat paws and the lining of her ears were beautifully clean and pink. Her eyes were lemon yellow with black pupils that grew large and round in the evening and narrowed to slits like a pencil stroke when she walked out in the sun.

Danny caught up with her. She arched her back and raised her tail and spat at him.

'Don't do that,' said Danny Fox. 'I only wanted to tell you that your master, the farmer, has lost you.'

'What's that to do with you?' she said.

'Nothing,' said Danny. 'But where are you going?' He remembered how Shaggy had told Swallow to follow her everywhere. He thought Swallow must have lost her too. 'Are you going to the town?'

'It's no business of yours,' said Lady Shiny, and spat at him again.

'Next time you spit, I'll bite you,' said Danny.

'If you bite me, I shall tell the Queen and she'll lock you up in her dungeon.'

'Do you know the Queen?' said Danny Fox, puzzled, with his head on one side. And Lady Shiny, the farmer's cat, was so proud of knowing the Queen that she gave away her secret.

'Of course I know the Queen,' she said grandly. 'I often go to the palace to play chess with her.'

'Who wins?' asked Danny.

'The Queen always wins.'

'That shows you are not much good at chess.'

When Lady Shiny heard Danny Fox say that, her pride was hurt still more and she burst out, miaouing and squawling, with her most secret secret. 'I don't play against the Queen,' she squawled. 'I help her to win. She taught me. She's my friend. She gives me a beautiful meal when the game is over.'

'How do you help her?' said Danny.

'I'm not telling you.'

'Then you're just boasting. A boastful Shiny Lady cat, who pretends to help the Queen.'

'She couldn't win without me,' screamed the cat.

'Near the end of the game, she strokes my head and I move the bishop with my paw and she wins.'

Then the cat looked crossly at Danny. She was sorry she had said so much, but hoped he did not understand. She bounded away, forgetting the wet grass and Danny followed her towards the town. He was worried. He could not understand what she meant about the bishop, and he did not know where to find Swallow.

6. The Bishop Chases Danny

As Danny Fox trotted after Lady Shiny, thinking 'Where can Swallow be?' he heard a sound of rustling in a green bushy thicket that stood in the middle of the field. He looked in, and there was Swallow wagging his tail.

'Quick,' said Danny. 'Lady Shiny's just jumped over that wall.'

'I know,' said Swallow. 'I've been watching her all morning. I hid in case she grew suspicious.' But when Danny told him she was going to the palace, he bounded from the thicket in a hurry, afraid of losing track of her. 'If she does get into the palace,' he said, 'how can I get in too?'

They ran fast across the fields, jumping each stone wall with a flying leap, and reached the market square just in time to see Lady Shiny stepping primly

up to the palace door. Finding it closed, she sat down on the doorstep to wait.

The whole market square was filled with stalls with brightly coloured canvas tops, some red, some blue, some yellow, some striped with all the colours of the rainbow, and it was easy for Swallow and Danny to hide. They dashed into the square and once they were under the first stall they could run all over the market without being seen, first under one stall, then another, watching people's feet and legs. Danny was looking for the fisherman's legs. He knew he must find him and show him the way to the dungeon. Swallow was watching Lady Shiny out of the corner of his eye, wherever he went. He could see the palace doorstep from the stalls and the lower part of the door, where she sat waiting.

Neither Danny Fox nor Swallow had ever been in such a noisy place before. The alleyways between the stalls were packed with people, talking, laughing, shouting, and the stall-holders were calling out to them, chanting the names of what they had to sell, like this:

'Ripe tomatoes. Ripe!'
'Cherries. Sweet cherries. Sweet!'
'Ripe strawberries!'
'Raspberries neat in a basket!'
'Jugs and teapots, bowls and pans!'
'Cups and saucers, patty-pans!'
'Jewels and bracelets safe in a casket!'

'Antique chessmen used by queens of old,
Now cheaply bought at thrice their weight
in gold.'

Danny Fox and Swallow were underneath the stall where the man was shouting 'Antique chessmen!', when Danny saw a pair of very fat legs done up in purple gaiters.

'That must be the Bishop,' he whispered to Swallow. 'Can you hear any keys go jingle-jangle in his tummy?'

'I can't even see his tummy,' said Swallow.

'Well,' said Danny. 'I'm going to make him run. Go ahead. Crawl under a few stalls and wait further down and listen.'

The Bishop was saying in a fine deep voice 'How much are these chessmen? I am playing chess with the Queen tonight and I must have something to give her in case I lose.'

'Three times their weight in gold, your Grace.'

'Then weigh them,' said the Bishop, 'and we'll see.' But all he saw was a streak of red lightning flashing round his legs. Danny Fox had come out from under the stall and was darting wildly in and out between the Bishop's legs. The Bishop drew back, thinking he would be bitten by a mad dog. It was only when Danny started to run, in full view of everyone between the rows of stalls, towards the palace, that he saw it was a fox.

'A fox! A fox! View-Hulloo!' the Bishop cried. And chased him as fast as he could. But he was fat and soon got out of breath. Swallow heard no jingle-jangle as he passed, nothing except his panting breath going 'Phoo-puff, phoo-puff, phoo-puff.' The stall-holders left their stalls and joined the chase and all the customers stopped looking at the things that were for sale and joined in too, until the market became a hunting field. They chased Danny Fox up and down between the stalls, knocking over trays of oranges and apples, squashing tomatoes and scattering cherries, stumbling and slipping and tripping one another up. Swallow ran beside them, underneath the stalls, keeping pace with the Bishop and listening for the jingle-jangle in his tummy. But he heard nothing except the same puffing and blowing. Danny Fox was just in front of the Bishop and a large crowd of people were running close behind, when at a corner by an ironmonger's stall, Danny caught his feet in a tangle of ropes and upset a pot of

white paint which burst and splashed over the ground. The Bishop leant down to grab him by the tail, and stopped so suddenly that all the people tumbled over him and knocked him to the ground. They all fell on top of him, laughing and shouting in a heap, and Danny Fox shook the ropes away and ran. He ran into the garden of the palace and hid in the hedge by the dustbins near the steps which led down to the dungeon.

He thought no one had seen him escape. The people were busy nursing bruised elbows and knees and helping the Bishop to his feet and dusting his clothes and fixing up his purple gaiters which had come loose. They did not think about Danny till later. But the fisherman, who had been watching the chase, and planning to rescue Danny, had seen him run behind the palace. He searched for him and found him by the dustbins.

Together they went down the slimy steps and the twisty staircase and along the damp dark passage, and peered through the rusty iron grating into the dungeon.

The fisherman called to the Princess and Danny barked. But there was no answer. The fisherman called again and Danny barked again and there was no answer. And once again, but still no answer.

'Are you sure this is the dungeon?' said the fisherman.

'Yes.'

'Perhaps she grew so hungry that she promised to dress up.'

'I don't think so,' said Danny. 'But they've taken her out of the dungeon, that's certain. And we'll have to find the reason why.'

The fisherman pushed the cloth full of fish and potatoes through the grating, hoping she would find them if she was brought back hungry and he and Danny climbed the stairs slowly, not knowing what to do next. When they reached the market square again, the fisherman picked Danny up and hid him under his ragged coat.

Lady Shiny was still waiting patiently by the front door of the palace for someone to open it and let her slip inside. Swallow was watching her from underneath the nearest market stall, which was the ironmonger's, where the paint had been spilt, and as soon as he saw the fisherman's legs he called quietly with a little yelp. The ironmonger looked up and down, not knowing where the sound came from, and while his head was turned away the fisherman put Danny down. Danny crept under the stall and hid with Swallow. The fisherman waited patiently near by.

'The Princess has gone from the dungeon,' whispered Danny. 'We'll have to get into the palace and find her.'

'But we'll be seen,' said Swallow.

'Let's roll in that white paint,' said Danny Fox, 'and they'll think we're spotty dogs.'

So one by one, while the ironmonger was busy with customers, they rolled in the patch of paint that had burst open till they looked like blotchy mongrels, red and white.

Danny Fox put his nose out from under the stall and tugged the fisherman's trousers.

'Go up to the palace and knock on the door and say you've got two dogs for sale,' he said.

The fisherman laughed.

'You're not to laugh,' said Danny. 'Just ask for the King. He's fond of dogs.'

So the fisherman walked up to the door of the palace with Danny Fox and Swallow at his heels, and everybody watching thought, 'What nice, obedient spotty dogs!'

Swallow was staring at Lady Shiny all the time. She did not like to be stared at. She spat at him. But would not leave her place by the palace door.

When the fisherman banged the huge gold knocker, Lady Shiny rubbed her head and neck against the doorpost, knowing that someone would answer and give her a chance to get in.

The under-under Chamberlain appeared and told the fisherman to go away.

'But I want to see the King,' the fisherman said. 'I have two dogs for sale.'

'You have no shoes on. You can't come in.' As the under-under Chamberlain spoke, Swallow saw Lady Shiny slip by his legs into the palace. He tried to jump forward but the door was slammed in his face.

Then the fisherman banged the knocker twice and the under Chamberlain appeared and said, 'Your trousers are tarry. You can't come in,' and slammed the door.

Then the fisherman banged three times and the Chamberlain himself appeared and said, 'Your shirt is torn. You can't come in.'

The fisherman banged four times and at last the Lord High Chamberlain stood in the doorway. 'Good gracious!' he said. 'Your feet are bare, your trousers tarry, your coat ragged, your shirt torn, and you haven't brushed your hair. Go away!'

'Then please take my dogs and show them to His Majesty the King,' the fisherman said.

The Lord High Chamberlain stared at Danny Fox

and Swallow. 'They are mongrels!' he shouted angrily. 'Take your nasty dogs away!'

The fisherman was just about to leave when the King came running down the corridor waving his sceptre with one hand and holding his crown to his head with the other. 'Dogs!' he cried. 'My dear Lord High Chamberlain, I can't believe my ears! You are sending dogs away?'

'I beg your pardon, your Majesty. I didn't think you'd like their blotchy spots. And they smell most dreadfully of paint.'

'That must be the latest dog shampoo,' said the King, looking lovingly at Danny and Swallow. 'You know nothing about dogs. These are Dalmatians – a new breed with red and white spots instead of black and white, much smaller and more cuddlesome. I can let them sleep on my bed. Are they house-trained?'

'They are palace-trained,' said the fisherman. 'At least they will be as soon as they get inside.'

'Wag your tail,' whispered Danny Fox to Swallow and they both wagged their tails and tried to smile. The King clapped his hands.

'Oh my dear Lord High Chamberlain,' he cried out laughing, 'have you ever seen Dalmatians with thick bushy tails before?'

'No, your Majesty.'

'Well, don't sound so gloomy. My dear daughter the Princess will be delighted. She needs cheering up. How much are they?'

'A halfpenny each,' said the fisherman.

'Send for the Lord High Treasurer,' said the King. The Lord High Treasurer came with five men to carry his sack of halfpennies and after one glance at the fisherman picked out two bent ones and handed them over. 'Thank you,' said the fisherman and went away, and Danny Fox and Swallow followed the King sedately into the Palace, trying to look like two spotty, good little dogs.

'What's "palace-trained"?' whispered Swallow, feeling nervous.

'It means you don't bite the Queen,' said Danny Fox.

7. What Funny Dalmations

'Come along my dear Dalmatians,' said the King, and Danny Fox and Swallow walked behind him as primly as they could down one long corridor and another and another until they reached a tiny room with silver walls and a thick black carpet.

'Better not sit down till the paint dries,' said Danny to Swallow in a whisper and then they had such a surprise that they forgot to be prim and jumped and barked with delight. The Princess was sitting at a little white ivory table, dressed in her royal robes, reading a book about chess.

'Quiet, dogs!' said the King. 'My darling daughter, I have just bought two Dalmatians. I thought they'd cheer you up.'

'Dalmatians?' said the Princess, laying down her book. 'What very funny Dalmatians!' She was staring at Danny and Swallow but did not know them at first.

'You can have them for company during the day,' said the King. 'But at night they'll sleep on my bed.'

Just at that moment, Danny Fox's ear began to itch, as it so often did, and not wanting to stain the carpet, he stood on three legs with his head on one

side to scratch it. 'Danny Fox is always scratching his ear,' the Princess thought, and then she saw the side of his face, which had no paint on it, and then she saw his beautiful thick bushy white-tipped tail. 'It's Dan ...' she shouted, but stopped herself in time and burst out laughing. 'Dalmatian. Yes,' said the King. 'I knew you would like them. You haven't laughed once since you came to the palace. Look after them for me, the sweet little things.' He went away and as soon as he closed the door behind him, they told her all that had happened.

'I see you had to give in,' said Danny Fox, 'and wear the grand clothes.'

The Princess said, 'It is only for a day. The Queen, my stepmother, promised me that if I put them on and won a game of chess against her in the evening, she would let me go home.'

'You won't be able to win,' said Danny.

'I always did when I was a child. She's not very good at chess.'

'That was before she taught Lady Shiny to help

81

her,' said Danny, and he told the Princess Lady Shiny's secret.

'Then as soon as I see my stepmother stroke Lady Shiny's head I'll take her paw in my hand,' the Princess said. 'And anyway, the Bishop's playing the first match. I'll be able to watch what happens.'

'Did you hear any keys go jingle-jangle in his tummy?' said Danny to Swallow.

'No. And he chased you like mad. I would have heard them.'

'What!' said the Princess and laughed. 'Did you think I meant the real bishop? The keys of the dungeon are in one of the chessmen – inside one of the two black bishops.'

'A black bishop?' said Danny, remembering Shaggy's riddle. 'Is that a man that isn't a man?'

'Yes. It's a chessman – not a real man.'

'Does it go jingle-jangle?'

'The Queen's one does. If you move it you can hear the keys inside.'

'Shaggy the Wild Cat said I'd find the keys by listening. She said,

"Inside a man that is not a man
You will hear a jingle-jangle that is not a bell."

Now I know what she meant.'

'Well anyway it doesn't matter now,' the Princess said. 'I am sure I shall win. They won't put me back in the dungeon.'

Danny Fox and Swallow had a day of bliss at the palace. First, the Princess took them into the garden to let the paint dry in the sun and they chased each other among the bushes and over the wide lawns till they tumbled head over heels into a strawberry bed. Then they ate many strawberries and the Princess ate a few. Then she took them to a greenhouse where they stood on their hind legs eating grapes, then to another greenhouse where she picked peaches for them. And then she said, 'Are you ready for dinner?' and led them back to the palace and into the banqueting hall.

'Be nice to the Queen, this time,' she said, so Danny and Swallow dashed up to her chair at the end of the table, put their paws on her lap and licked her face. She screamed.

'They are trying to make friends,' said the King to calm her. 'Dalmatians are so sweet-natured!'

'They look more like wild animals to me,' said the Queen.

'That's because they are thin,' said the King and he asked the Head Butler to lay twenty dishes of food on the floor, ten courses for Swallow and ten for Danny Fox, starting with soup and ending with trifle. Danny thought of Mrs Doxie Fox – how hungry she must be – and wished he could turn her into a Dalmatian. Swallow thought of Shaggy the Wild Cat and planned to bring some food home to her. But they both knew they must stay in the palace until the game of chess was over, so after dinner they jumped on to the King's throne and slept together till the evening. Lady Shiny was curled up on the Queen's throne beside them, with one eye open, pretending to be asleep, pretending not to notice them, but when the time came for the chess match, she yawned and jumped to the floor. The sound woke them and they followed her out of the throne room.

The chess match was played in the small silver room with the black carpet and although the sun had not yet quite gone down, heavy curtains were drawn across the window as if it was the middle of the night. The room was lit by three candles, two dim ones on the mantelpiece and, on the ivory table where the chessboard was laid out, a beeswax candle so bright and clear that Swallow thought the planet Venus had come into the room. He growled at it loudly, forgetting palace manners.

'Those dogs of yours!' said the Queen to the King. 'Drive them out. They'll put the Bishop off his game.'

But luckily the Bishop was fond of dogs and asked if they might stay. 'They have delightful spots,' he said. 'And those thick bushy tails remind me of some other animal. I can't remember what. Do you know, my dear Queen, I almost caught a fox by the tail this morning in the market.'

'A fox near the palace!' cried the Queen. 'Dear me, I hope not!'

Danny tried to hide his tail by sitting on it, afraid that the Bishop might remember more, but he chose a place where he had a good view of the chessboard, near the Queen's side of it where the light from the candle was less dazzling. Swallow sat down not far from Lady Shiny who was perched, with her eyes half closed, pretending to see nothing, on a special stool which the Queen had ordered to be made for her exactly the same height as the table so that she could reach the chessmen with her paw.

The game between the Bishop and the Queen began. From where he sat, Danny Fox could see every one of the black and white squares of the chessboard and all the chessmen standing on the squares like two armies facing each other – a white army on the Queen's side and a black army on the Bishop's. In front of each stood the pawns, the smallest of the chessmen. They were like soldiers. And at the back of each army were the knights, the castles and the chess bishops, and, tallest and most important of all, the chess king and the chess queen. The real Queen and the real Bishop moved their chessmen from square to square, taking prisoners from each other until there were very few chessmen left on the board.

Near the end of the game the Princess bent down to Danny and whispered, 'Watch carefully. If the white army can trap the black king, my stepmother will win. But the Bishop has placed his black bishop on guard and I think he'll be able to win.'

At that moment, Danny Fox saw her stepmother, the Queen, push the bright candle away from her close to the real Bishop's eyes. It dazzled him. He was too polite to complain but put up his hand to shade his eyes and quickly the Queen stroked Lady Shiny's forehead and she stretched out a silent paw and moved the black bishop away from the square where it was guarding the king. The real Bishop, dazzled by the light, saw nothing, and soon he lost the game. He presented the Queen with the set of antique chessmen, which he had bought in the market, and smiled at her and sighed.

'My dear Queen,' said the Bishop, 'Am I growing stupider at chess or are you growing more and more skilful? I used to be able to beat you sometimes.'

The Queen took Lady Shiny on her lap and stroked her lovingly. Lady Shiny purred. The King looked proudly at the Queen and said, 'It is my dear Queen who grows better and better at chess. She can even beat the doctor these days.'

'Well, I can win against the doctor,' said the Bishop, 'but not against our dear Queen any more. No one can beat her.'

'And I know why!' said Danny Fox to himself, staring hard at Lady Shiny.

'Now,' said the Bishop, to the Princess, in a kindly tone of voice, 'please let me stay and watch you play your mother. You are very good at chess.'

'I used to be when I was at school,' the Princess

said, getting up from her easy chair and approaching the chess table, but her mother yawned and said, 'I am tired. We'll play our game tomorrow night, my daughter. But remember the conditions?'

The Princess could not very well forget them. She repeated them aloud to her mother: 'If I win, you will let me go home to my husband and live in the fisherman's house. If you win, I'll have to stay here in the dungeon and live on dry bread and water.'

'No, no, no, you silly girl!' The Queen tapped her lightly on the cheek with her sceptre. 'If I win, you will wear proper clothes and behave like a proper Princess and bring your husband here and both of you live like proper people in a proper palace with proper rooms and proper servants and a proper King, your father, and a proper Queen, your mother, and a proper garden, and a proper dustbin, and a proper back door and a proper front door, and a proper Lazy Parlour and a proper, proper, proper, proper ...' But the Queen was so tired she could not think of any more proper things. 'Let's go to bed,' she said.

'But you won't send me back to the dungeon tonight?' the Princess said, afraid.

'Of course not, my dear girl, if you promise to wear a proper nightdress.'

The Princess promised.

'And a proper dress tomorrow.'

The Princess promised. But only for tomorrow. Then the Queen gave Lady Shiny a beautiful meal and opened the window for her to jump out and run home to the farmer's house where she lived. Danny was ready to jump out after her, but the Queen closed the window before he could reach it. The King held the door of the chess-room open to let the Queen pass through on her way to bed. 'Come along dogs,' he called to Danny and Swallow. 'Come upstairs. You may sleep on my bed.' He held his candle high to show them the way to the staircase. But of course they did not want to be shut in the Royal Bedroom for the night, and, whispering to Swallow to follow, Danny rushed past the staircase and turned quickly into the dark passage that led to the Luxurious Parlour, the Little Parlour and the Lazy Parlour. All this part of the palace was unlit, for it was late at night, and the King could not see where they had gone. 'Ah well,' he said. 'They'll be quite

safe. They can't get out of the palace and go astray.'
He went to bed.

Danny Fox and Swallow burrowed deep under the
laziest cushions of the Lazy Parlour.

'Keep your tail in,' said Danny, 'in case they
search for us.'

Swallow felt lazier and lazier and Danny Fox felt
lazier and lazier and soon they and everybody else in
the palace fell sound asleep.

8. Danny Fox Learns Magic

When Swallow woke in the very early morning he jumped from the cushions and put his nose to every window in the Lazy Parlour. Danny Fox was watching him, but did not get up.

'You may as well lie down again,' said Danny. 'All the windows in the palace are closed, and the back door is locked and the front door is locked and bolted and fixed with chains.'

'Then how shall we get out?' said Swallow in despair. 'We can't spend another day being nice Dalmatians. It's so *boring*,' he howled.

'Sssh!' said Danny. Swallow crept up to him and whispered, 'Besides we must see Shaggy. I promised to tell her everything that I saw Lady Shiny do.'

'It will be all right,' said Danny Fox. 'Lie down again and when I leave the Lazy Parlour, follow me.'

They lay on the cushions pricking up their ears at every tiny sound – a moth on the window pane, a mouse in the wainscot – until at last Danny Fox heard sly footsteps, tip-toeing down the marble staircase of the palace. Tip toe, tip toe, tip toe, slowly and stealthily, step by step, down came the Queen's High Mixer of Dainty Cakes on his way to the baker's shop across the square. At every step he paused to listen, afraid that the Queen might have heard him.

At last he reached the front door and began to unfasten the bolts and chains and lock as quietly as he could. This was the moment Danny Fox was waiting for. With Swallow behind him, he ran from the Lazy Parlour along the passage that led to the front door. The Queen's High Mixer of Dainty Cakes left the door open as usual as he ran across the square and Danny Fox and Swallow slipped out unseen and away across the fields towards home.

Swallow never stopped, nor once looked back, till he came to his den at the top of the mountain where Shaggy the Wild Cat was curled up asleep on the Queen's starry petticoat. Danny Fox never stopped, nor once looked back, until he reached his den where Mrs Doxie Fox and Choke were waiting for him.

When Mrs Doxie Fox sniffed Danny's coat in the darkness of the cave, she smelt paint and felt patches of stiff bristles in his soft fur. Choke thought a stranger had come into the den and was afraid.

'Last time you came home, you were smothered in the Queen's best scent,' said Mrs Doxie Fox. 'Is this the King's?'

'It's one of my best tricks,' said Danny Fox. 'My tricks have come back to me at last.'

'I knew they would. But I wish they didn't smell so nasty,' said Mrs Doxie Fox, and she tried to lick the paint off.

'No, don't,' said Danny. 'Can't you see I'm a Dalmatian?'

'What's that?' said Mrs Doxie Fox.

'It's the name of a very lucky breed of dog, who has ten course dinners and goes to sleep on the throne in the afternoon and to bed with the King and Queen at night.'

'I don't think I like Dalmatians,' said Choke.

'Never mind,' said Danny. 'It's only till tonight. Tomorrow I shall be a fox again.'

He looked after Choke while her mother went to find something to eat, then ran up the mountain to Swallow's den.

Shaggy the Wild Cat was sitting upright on the starry petticoat inside the cave, her forelegs straight and close together, her paws hidden by her tail

which curled over them round the front of her body.
Swallow was lying against the wall watching her.
She looked beautiful and mysterious in the half-light
of the den, like Bast, the cat-goddess of Egypt. She
did not even glance at Danny Fox when he crawled
in. But Swallow rose to greet him.

They told Shaggy the Wild Cat how Lady Shiny
had helped the Queen to win and how the Queen had
dazzled the Bishop with a candle that was as bright
as the planet Venus.

'The Queen will dazzle the Princess too,' said
Danny Fox.

'Lady Shiny will help the Queen again tonight,'
said Swallow, 'unless you tell us what to do.'

'Why don't you blow the candle out?' said Shaggy.

'Foxes can't blow,' said Danny.

'Then spit at it and put it out.'

'Foxes can't spit,' said Danny.

'Then knock it over.'

'The Queen would stop the game and light it.'

'You'd better come with us,' said Swallow. 'You can spit.'

Shaggy seemed to take no notice. She washed behind her ears while Swallow whimpered with impatience. But Danny Fox sat quietly waiting for her to speak. He knew she was a wise old cat and that she could help them. At last she said, 'You must spoil Lady Shiny's magic by a trick.'

'But you said magic was better than a trick,' said Swallow.

'So it is. But foxes only know tricks.'

'What is magic?' said Danny.

'If you could make Lady Shiny think of something else, without touching her, just at the moment when the Queen strokes her forehead, that would be magic,' said Shaggy the Wild Cat. 'If, without moving or making a sound, you could make her jump down from her stool, that would be very strong magic.' And that was all she would say.

It was daylight when Danny Fox and Swallow left her and walked together down the mountain. Swallow suggested catching hundreds of fleas in a salt cellar and sprinkling them over Lady Shiny, just before the game began, to make her fidget and scratch. He thought of dropping bits of juicy fish on the floor beside her or getting the Princess to bring in a bowl of thick cream, but Danny Fox said, 'No, she's too well fed to be tempted. It must be something she can't resist whether she's hungry or not.'

'A bird,' said Swallow, 'but how could we catch one? A mouse or a rat?'

'That's it,' said Danny. 'If she suddenly saw a rat moving, she would never think of chess.'

'But how could we get one and bring it alive to the palace?'

Danny Fox walked on with his nose to the ground as he often did when he was thinking. Then suddenly he jumped with joy, barking and twisting his body in the air. He landed on all four feet beside Swallow.

'Run down to the farm as quickly as you can,' he said. 'And go to the straw stacks where the rats live. Tear out an old nest that smells of rats and take it to the fisherman's. I'll meet you there.'

Danny Fox ran home and called for Mrs Doxie Fox and Choke.

'But where are you taking us?' said Mrs Doxie Fox.

'It's a secret. It's one of my tricks.' And he ran so fast down the mountain that she had to pick up Choke and carry her in her mouth.

They met Swallow outside the fisherman's house. He was carrying a bundle of straw which smelt strongly of rats. Choke liked the smell and wanted to play with it. 'Swallow has brought a special scent for you,' said Danny Fox. 'Let her roll in it, Swallow, till she smells like a rat.' Then he asked the fisherman to make a little box with air holes at the side and a door at one end, and to write on it, 'A Present for the Princess'. They lined it with the ratty straw and, after she had had her feed, Choke crept inside and lay down to sleep. She liked her new nest. It was cosy and smelt lovely and she dreamt of chasing rats and mice.

The fisherman made collars and leads out of string for Danny Fox and Swallow, and with Choke in her box beneath his arm he led them back to the palace as though they were dogs. They told Mrs Doxie Fox to run across the fields, in case the farmer saw her on the road, and to hide till they called her in the hedge by the palace dustbins.

When they came to the market square they saw a huge notice board with a crowd of people staring at

LOST
TWO PRIZE DALMATIANS
SPOTTED RED AND WHITE
THEY COST ONE HALFPENNY EACH
BUT ARE THE PRICELESS PROPERTY
OF HIS MAJESTY THE KING
WHO WILL GIVE THE FINDER
ONE HUNDRED POUNDS REWARD

it. The letters were so big and bright that the fisherman could read it from a distance. 'Good gracious!'
he said, and he read aloud:

LOST

TWO PRIZE DALMATIANS

SPOTTED RED AND WHITE

THEY COST ONE HALFPENNY EACH

BUT ARE THE PRICELESS PROPERTY

OF HIS MAJESTY THE KING

WHO WILL GIVE THE FINDER

ONE HUNDRED POUNDS REWARD

When the people saw the fisherman walk up to the
palace door, with two little dogs spotted red and
white, they gave a great shout, 'He's found them!
Oh, he's lucky.' And the King heard the shout from
inside the palace and came running to open the door
without any servants to help him. He had never had
to open this huge door before and instead of turning
the handle he began to fumble with the hinges, calling out frantically 'Don't go away. If you've got
my little dogs, don't go. I'll get it open in a minute.
Carpenter! Carpenter! Where is the Royal
Carpenter?'

The Royal Carpenter came running with his bag
of tools.

The King pointed at the golden hinges and said
'Undo these screws. The door has stuck.'

'Very good, your Majesty,' said the Royal Carpenter. 'But you must stand to one side. The door will fall down and it is very heavy.'

'I don't care if it falls down,' cried the King. 'I only want to get it open quickly.'

'The quickest way to open it, your Majesty, is this way,' the Royal Carpenter said, undoing the bolts and chains, turning the door knob gently and pulling the door wide open.

'Oh, you are the best and quickest carpenter I ever had,' said the King. 'I shall give you a special reward. Oh, where did you find them?' he said to the fisherman. 'I've been out of my wits with worry.'

'They came to my house,' the fisherman said.

'Homesick, the poor little things. Dalmatians really are the most loving of all dogs. Well, I'll keep them one more day and if they are still unhappy here tomorrow, I shall let them go.'

He called for the Royal Treasurer who came with five men to carry his sacks of pound notes, but the fisherman would not take the reward. The King was upset. He wanted to keep his promise. But still the fisherman said 'No.'

'Then, if you won't take money,' said the King, 'What else would you like? What is it you want most in all the world.'

The fisherman nearly said 'The Princess,' but knew that would be a mistake.

'Well,' said the King, 'there must be something you need.'

'A new rope for my boat.'

So the Royal Ropemaker came carrying coils of rope and gave him the longest, strongest coil he could find. The fisherman said 'Thank you,' and gave the King the box with Choke asleep inside it. 'Please give this to the Princess,' he said. 'It is a secret, your Majesty. Tell no one else.'

'Oh, thank you,' said the King. Then, smiling with joy, he led Danny Fox and Swallow into the palace again.

9. Danny Grabs the Black Bishop

Danny Fox and Swallow followed the King sedately down one long corridor and another and another until they reached the tiny room with silver walls and a black carpet. The Princess was sitting as before at the ivory table, dressed in her royal robes reading the book about chess, but this time they remembered not to jump and bark. 'We can sit down,' said Danny, and they kept quiet until the King had handed her her present and left the room.

Then Danny Fox said to the Princess, 'You mustn't open it until the evening. You must hold it on your lap during the chess match, and as soon as the Queen pushes the candle towards your eyes, hold it up on a level with the table and open the door in front.'

'But what is it?' said the Princess. 'It smells like an animal.'

'A magic animal,' said Danny Fox. 'A secret! Take it to the dark yew hedge where Mrs Doxie Fox is hiding.'

The Princess carried her mysterious present out and laid it down by the hedge. Danny and Swallow came with her, then led her away from the hiding place. Once they had walked away, Mrs Doxie Fox

found Choke. The fisherman had made a simple latch for the door of the box and she opened it with her nose to let the baby out. She looked after Choke all day in her hiding-place while the Princess walked about the garden watching Danny and Swallow as they played on the sunny lawn, running and jumping and bumping and biting and fighting each other in fun, rumbling and grumbling with growls and howls and tumbling into flower-beds.

Then they went into the palace for their midday feast, and saved plenty to take out to Mrs Doxie Fox. And then they went to sleep on the King's throne as before while Lady Shiny pretended to sleep on the Queen's throne beside them.

When the time for the chess match came, the King led Danny Fox and Swallow into the silver room where the Queen and the Bishop were chatting as they waited for the Princess to come, in her beautiful royal clothes, and play her fatal game of chess.

Swallow sat down by the fireplace trying to look like a good Dalmatian. Lady Shiny was on her stool by the ivory chess table with her eyes half shut. Danny Fox kept his eyes wide open. The King walked round and round the room. He felt nervous. He wanted the Princess to win.

When the Princess came she was so beautiful that everybody, even Lady Shiny, looked up at her. She was carrying her present, the secret box with the magic animal in it. Even the Princess did not know that the magic animal was Danny Fox's baby – Choke. She laid the box on her lap as she sat down at the chess table opposite her stepmother the Queen, and she placed her army on the board to face the Queen's. She had the black army, the Queen the white. As she placed her black bishop on its square, she looked at

Danny and shook it a little. He heard the jingle-jangle and knew that the keys to the dungeon were hidden inside it.

Then the Queen lit the candle that was as bright as the planet Venus.

Danny Fox looked sharply at Lady Shiny who was watching him out of the corner of one eye, and then he crept under the table to make sure that Choke was safe in her box on the Princess's lap. When the game began he sat near Lady Shiny.

Lady Shiny sat as still as ever on her stool, but soon her whiskers began to twitch and her dainty pink nose to quiver. She smelt a rat, but she thought to herself, 'There can't be a rat in the silver chess-room. It must be a dream.'

When Choke woke up and felt lonely for her mother, half way through the game, Lady Shiny's white ears began to move. Danny saw their pink linings by the flame of the bright candle as they moved this way and that trying to find out where the sound of rustling straw came from, and he saw her twitching whiskers shining silvery in the light.

Lady Shiny thought, 'There can't be straw in the silver chess-room and there can't be a rat. But I can hear straw rustling and I can smell a rat.' She tried her best to keep still.

It was nearly the end of the game by now. The Princess's black army had taken many prisoners from the Queen's white army. There were only a few white chessmen left on the board and the Princess felt happy. Her army was in a strong position. Her king was safe behind a black bishop. She knew she could win and go home to her house on the beach and live with the fisherman again.

Then suddenly the Queen pushed the candle so close to her eyes that it almost burnt her eyelashes She drew back quickly and opened Choke's box. Choke, who was longing for her mother, ran out at once along the edge of the chess table just at the very moment when the Queen was stroking Lady Shiny's forehead. Lady Shiny forgot all about stretching out her silent paw to move the black bishop away from the square where he was on guard. She smelt a strong smell of rats and thought she saw one – a very large chocolate coloured rat, with thick fur on its tail, running along the edge of the table. She sprang at it with all her claws ready. But Choke jumped to the floor just in time and ran to hide under Danny Fox's tummy. And the candle that was as bright as the planet Venus fell and went out. In her excitement Lady Shiny had knocked it over.

It had all happened so quickly that the Queen did not see Choke. She only saw Lady Shiny knock the candle over but, instead of being cross with her for that, she shrieked out at the Princess, 'What are you doing, you silly girl? You knocked the candle over! How can I see to play? You are trying to cheat!'

'No, stepmother. Let us light the candle again.'

They put it back on the table and lit it, but Lady Shiny was on the floor searching for the rat she thought she had seen. The Princess's black bishop was still guarding her black king and the Queen could not possibly win. Soon the Princess trapped the Queen's white king and won the match.

The Queen could not believe it. First she closed her eyes and then she opened them. Then she opened her mouth and closed it with a snap like the lid of a box. Then she shrieked at the Princess. Her voice was like the sound of somebody smashing a plate on the floor.

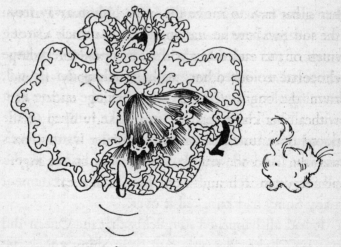

'You cheated,' she shrieked. Her face grew red and her hair stood up like a porcupine's quills, and she shouted at the King, 'The Princess cheated! Back to the dungeon with her! Back to the dungeon with her! Back to the dungeon!'

'But I did not cheat,' the Princess said. 'I won the game, that's all. And you promised to let me go back to the fisherman's house if I won.'

'The Bishop said no one can beat me,' screamed the Queen. 'Do you think you know better than the Bishop? You wicked girl, you cheated me. You cheated!'

'I am sure she didn't cheat!' began the Bishop.

'We must let her go home,' said the King. But the Queen rushed out of the room to call the soldiers.

The Princess sat with her elbows on the ivory table resting her face on her hands to hide her tears. Danny Fox and Swallow sat unhappily on the black carpet, whispering to each other, and the King and the Bishop whispered to each other, walking unhappily up and down the room. Choke was nestling under her brother Swallow's legs for safety. Lady Shiny had stalked out into the corridor twitching her tail because she felt cross with the Queen, who in her anger had forgotten to bring her her beautiful meal.

When the Queen came back with six soldiers Danny Fox crept up to the Princess and said, 'We'll save you by tomorrow. I've thought of a trick that will rescue you.' She stopped crying and even when the soldiers fastened on her chains and led her away towards the dungeon she did not cry.

The trick Danny Fox had thought of came from his idea of Shaggy the Wild Cat's magic: if he could make the Queen think of something else while she was putting the chessmen away, he would grab the black bishop that held the keys.

There was only one set of keys to the dungeon and only one way in – by the winding staircase outside the palace. The soldiers led the Princess out through the front door, round to the back of the palace, down the dismal staircase and along the underground passage to the grating where they waited for the Queen to come and unlock the two padlocks.

Danny Fox and Swallow sat watching the Queen as she put away the chessmen, white and black, and locked them into an ebony casket. Danny Fox was watching for a chance to grab the black bishop, but she clutched it firmly in one hand as she put the others away, then carried it briskly from the room, jingle-jangle down the long corridor and out of the front door. The King and the Bishop followed her and Danny and Swallow followed them all with Choke pattering along behind as fast as she could go. Her mother, Mrs Doxie Fox, had been hiding by the dustbins under the dark yew hedge all this time and now crept out to bring her into the hiding-place and cuddle her and feed her. It was dark. The moon had not yet risen. The King, the Bishop, Danny Fox and Swallow waited at the top of the winding staircase for the Queen to come up after locking the Princess in.

When she came Danny Fox barked at her furiously and long – 'woo-oo, woo-oo, woo-oo!'

'That's a fox's bark,' cried the Bishop.

'It's only my dear Dalmatian,' said the King.

'A dog's bark is quite different,' said the Bishop.

The Queen shrieked, 'A fox! A fox in my garden. Help!' and the soldiers tried to slash Danny Fox and Swallow with their swords, but it was so dark that no one could see them. No one could even see their red and white spots.

Then Danny tugged the Queen's skirt with his teeth and ran away. Then Swallow tugged the other side of it and tore a piece of golden cloth off. They ran in circles round and round the garden, rushing back to bark at the Queen and away again and the soldiers were never quick enough for them. But when Danny barked again quite close in the dark the Queen knew where he was. 'It's over there,' she shouted to the soldiers. 'Can't you throw something at it?' she yelled, and without knowing what she was doing she threw the only thing she had in her hand – the black bishop.

Something hit Danny Fox on the side of his head and bounced off on to the grass. He could smell it. It smelt of the beautifully perfumed hand of the Queen. He found it at once and ran away through the town with the black bishop in his mouth. The soldiers chased him. The King and Queen and the Bishop went indoors and when all was quiet Mrs Doxie Fox and Choke and Swallow set out for home.

10. Danny Fox Saves the Princess

Danny Fox knew that the soldiers would chase him. If he ran home they would follow him to his den and Mrs Doxie Fox and Choke would be in danger. So he ran from the town in the opposite direction out into hilly country, which led up to a strange part of the mountain where he did not know his way. But in spite of feeling lost he was not at all afraid, because the soldiers in their big black boots were slow. He trotted along quietly with his ears turned back to listen for their footsteps. They were running for all their might, but grew further and further away. At last he could hear them no longer. All this time, he had the black bishop in his mouth.

Danny Fox did not know it, but the soldiers had turned back to the palace to ask the Royal Huntsmen to ride out on their horses and chase him, and now the Royal Hunting Dogs were loosed from their kennels and followed the scent of his paws. The Royal Hunting Dogs led the horsemen through the town and faster up into the hilly country and faster and faster until they came close enough for Danny Fox to catch their scent on the air.

Still holding the black bishop in his teeth, he ran for

his life uphill. He could hear the dogs yelping behind him. He ran fast, but their long, thin legs ran faster still. Now they were so close that he could hear their breath – panting, panting, nearer and nearer to his tail. Only a trick could save him. He turned sharply to the right. The dogs were slower in turning. He came to a steep bank and jumping down it, found himself in a narrow lane deep between high banks. He ran along it and felt safer – until he heard the dogs behind him once again. They too had jumped down the bank, with the men and horses after them.

And now the sun rose, letting the horsemen see him in the early morning light. They called to their dogs to run faster and their horses' hoofs clattered on the stony lane. Danny Fox thought he was done for, until after turning a bend he saw a hump-back bridge before him where the lane crossed a river. Here he was out of sight of the horsemen for a mom-

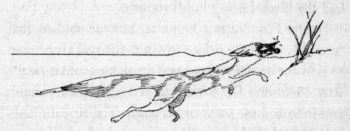

ent. Instead of crossing the bridge he leapt into the river and swam, but not straight across. Danny Fox was too clever to do that. He swam down the river and climbed out on the far bank a hundred yards away. The dogs lost his scent at the bridge and when they found it leading to the riverbank, of course they swam straight across and wandered up and down the far bank searching for it. Unluckily they found it and Danny soon heard them behind him again. His trick had not saved him. He knew he must think of another. But at least it had given him time.

He was running uphill and soon the dogs gained on him. This time he turned sharply to the left, to delay them, and jumped down into the lane again. But the dogs and horsemen jumped after him and soon came closer and closer to his tail. He was very tired by now. Then, turning a corner of this lane that led up the mountain, he saw his way blocked by a flock of sheep, so many sheep that they filled the lane from side to side. The Royal Hunting Dogs were close to him again. The banks of the lane were too steep to climb at this place and the sheep walked slowly, as they always do, following their shepherd. Danny Fox saw no way of escape. But all in a second he thought of a trick, He pushed his way into the middle of the flock of sheep and walked slowly along at their pace. Their wide woolly backs hid him perfectly. Their hundreds of feet, smelling strongly of sheep, hid the scent of his four little fox's feet, and the Royal Hunting Dogs stopped, wandering about and sniffing everywhere, not knowing where he had disappeared to. The Hunting Dogs went by scent, not sight, and all the horsemen saw when they reached the turning

of the lane was a huge flock of sheep walking slowly after their old shepherd.

The horsemen and dogs turned back and Danny walked on among the sheep until they reached their pasture high up on the mountain and spread out to graze, leaving him in the open in full view of the shepherd. The shepherd stared after him as he ran away and said, 'A spotty fox! They'll laugh at me when I get home this evening and tell them I've seen that.' He sat down on a rock to eat his breakfast which he had brought with him in a knapsack. The sun was shining now and had changed the close-cropped grass from its night-time black to a beautiful day-time green. Each blade of grass glistened with drops of dew and hanging between some blue wild orchids the shepherd saw spiders' webs sprinkled with dew – tiny nets made of silvery thread. This was the best time of day for the shepherd, to have his breakfast all alone in the early morning, sitting on a rock, while his sheep spread out before him feeding peacefully. He watched the white clouds too.

Danny Fox had had a good rest walking with the sheep, but he could not hurry because he did not know which way to go. He loped. He went loping away out of sight of the shepherd, loping along and along all alone not knowing where he was. He trotted on the mountain this way and that and only put the black bishop down once, to drink at a bubbling spring. As he was drinking he heard a fox bark, far

far away in the distance. He looked up and listened, then drank again. The fox barked again and now he knew the voice. It was Mrs Doxie Fox calling him.

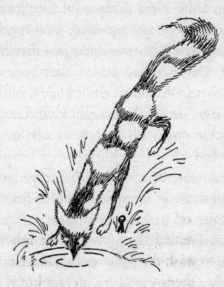

She had reached their den safely with Swallow and Choke in the middle of the night and after hours and hours without a sign of Danny she was afraid he had been caught. She went on barking and listening and barking.

Danny Fox began to gallop uphill and downhill, through thickets of bushes and over long stretches of purple heather, faster and faster towards the place her voice came from. He heard another bark which he knew was Swallow's and at last he saw in the distance the hawthorn bush, the beautiful thorny green bush that hid the entrance to their cave. He galloped down the mountain to it. He rushed through it and lay down panting on the earthy floor of the den between Swallow and Mrs Doxie Fox and Choke. He dropped the black bishop on the floor and his pink tongue hung out quivering between his white teeth. Mrs Doxie Fox and Choke and Swallow licked his face.

Danny Fox had a long rest now. He told Swallow that they must wait till midnight before they tried to rescue the Princess, until after everybody in the palace had gone to bed.

Swallow was disappointed. 'When can we stop being Dalmatians?' he said, trying to lick his white spots of paint off.

Late that evening they went to the fisherman and asked him to wash the paint away. He scrubbed them and scrubbed them with paraffin rags but it took him

almost till midnight to make their furry coats look red and beautiful again. The smell of paraffin was worse than paint and the fisherman told them to swim in the sea. The salt sea washed the smell away. Then they all set out for the palace. The fisherman carried the black bishop hidden in his trouser pocket and at every step he took they heard a jingle-jangle. Mrs Doxie Fox walked after them with Choke. She wanted to keep as near as possible to Danny Fox and help him if she could.

When they reached the palace and came to the steps of the dungeon they had a horrid shock. The Queen had placed her six soldiers there to guard the palace all night. She knew very well that whoever had stolen the keys would come back to let the Princess out, and she believed that after one more night in that nasty place the Princess would give in. But the Princess felt sure Danny Fox would rescue her, and she was not hungry, because she had found the parcel wrapped in cloth which the fisherman had pushed through the bars. The potatoes and fish were cold by then of course, but still fresh.

Danny Fox smelt the soldiers before they saw him, and stood still a little way off. The fisherman and the other foxes stood behind him.

Danny, whispering, said, 'Hide.' The fisherman hid behind the dark yew hedge and Swallow, Choke and Mrs Doxie Fox beneath it. Danny Fox saw several dead twigs of yew lying on the ground. Their bark was almost black. He picked up a short thick one and walked in front of the soldiers, curling up his lips to let them see this black bit of wood between his white teeth. The first soldier shouted, at once, 'The black bishop! He's got the black bishop!' and started to chase him. The others remained on guard.

'Call your brothers,' whispered Danny to Swallow as he ran past the dark yew hedge, 'and tell them to do what I'm doing.'

From under the hedge, Swallow watched him run away with the first soldier after him. Then he crept out on to the lawn and smelled the wind. He wagged his tail with pleasure when he found that the wind was blowing from behind the palace, towards the sea and the mountain where all the foxes lived. He knew it would carry his voice to them. He pointed his nose to the ground and uttered a long 'Yow-woo-ee, yoo-wo-wo-wo-oo-ee,' which meant, 'Lick and Chew come quickly and bring your wives to help!'

Meanwhile Danny Fox was running in wide circles, never far from the palace. He was not running fast. There was no need. And every now and then he sat down to let the soldier catch up with him, or nearly catch up. As soon as the soldier came near enough to see the black stick between Danny's teeth Danny Fox would start off again, leading him further away from the palace in wider and wider circles. And all this time Lick and his wife and Chew and his wife were galloping over the fields by the short-cut to the town, leaping the walls all four of them in the air like flying foxes, until they reached their youngest brother Swallow, their sister Choke and Mrs Doxie Fox their mother, and lay down beside them panting under the dark yew hedge.

While they were getting their breath back Swallow picked up a black, dead twig of yew and whispering to the others to watch him and do as he did, one by one in turn, he walked in front of the soldiers showing them the black piece of wood he held between his white teeth.

The second soldier shouted, 'The black bishop! That fox is back again!' And at once he began to chase Swallow, thinking he was chasing the same

fox that his friend had chased before. With the black stick in his mouth Swallow ran round in wider and wider circles, always slowing down to make sure that the second soldier did not lose sight of him.

Chew's fur was red like Swallow's and now he walked in front of the soldiers with a black stick between his white teeth. The third soldier raced after him thinking he was the same fox that his comrades had chased. Then Lick came with his beautiful red coat and a black stick between his white teeth, and his red tongue hanging out beneath it because he was still panting, and led the fourth soldier away from the dungeon in wider and wider circles. Then his wife came and led the fifth soldier away. Then Chew's wife came and led the last away – the sixth soldier who ran and ran to try to catch her, believing that she was carrying the black bishop in her mouth.

So at last there was no one on guard. All six soldiers were chasing all six foxes, each thinking there was only one fox, and only the fisherman and Mrs Doxie Fox and Choke were left by the dark yew hedge.

When all was quiet they crept out. The fisherman ran down to the dungeon, took the black bishop from his pocket, unscrewed its head as though it was a pepperpot, took out the two keys, undid the padlocks one by one, and helped the Princess up into the garden. The other foxes had all come back, leaving the soldiers searching for them through the woods.

The Princess and the fisherman hugged each other for so long that Danny said 'Hurry! The soldiers will come back!' The Princess bent down and kissed him. Then she saw Lick, then Chew, then Swallow, then Mrs Lick whose fur was so pale that she looked white in the moonlight, then Chew's wife whose fur was almost black. When she saw Mrs Doxie Fox and

Choke, she took Choke in her arms to cuddle her and carry her home. Mrs Doxie Fox kept close to her as they left the palace, looking up always to see that her baby was safe, and the fisherman walked beside them.

And they all went home across the fields in the moonlight, with a warm summer breeze behind them ruffling the fisherman's black curls and the fur of the foxes, and lifting the long yellow strands of the Princess's hair to blow the smell of the dank, dark dungeon away.

They walked in single file – first the fisherman, then the Princess, with Choke, then the seven foxes trotting one behind another, their shadows dancing on the moonlit grass. Swallow came last. He was dragging a heavy sack with him and could not keep pace with the others.

'I can see foxes on the ground,' said Choke, 'and foxes in the sky.'

'The foxes in the sky are wispy clouds,' the Princess said, 'floating along in the breeze.'

'There's a boat on the sand,' said Choke, when they reached the fisherman's house, 'and another boat in the sky.'

'The boat in the sky is a large white cloud,' the Princess said, as she handed her to her mother. But Choke was still only a baby. She did not understand.

'Now I know you will be safe,' she said, 'because I can see the Queen far away in the sky. She is sailing past the moon, with her crown on, in a ship.'

They all looked up and saw a long cloud with curved ends. An upright figure, plump as the Queen, seemed to be sitting on it. For a moment, it covered the moon and they were in darkness.

'Thank you for seeing such marvellous sights,' the Princess said. 'And, anyway, I know I shall be safe, so long as Danny Fox is living on the mountain near our house. The Queen knows now that he's too clever for her. She will not try to capture me again.' Then she kissed all the foxes goodnight and went into her house with the fisherman.

Chew and his wife, who was dark as the night, walked on along the beach, round the foot of the mountain towards their den on the far side by the sea. Lick and his wife, who was fair as the moon, ran fast

up the mountain to their den at the top. Danny Fox and Mrs Doxie Fox climbed home more slowly. Danny was tired after all his adventures and she was carrying Choke in her mouth. Swallow was last, and slowest, because he had to climb the mountain backwards dragging the heavy sack up to his den where Shaggy the Wild Cat was waiting for him.

'What is that?' said Shaggy, sniffing at the sack.

'It's fishy scraps and dainty cakes from the dustbins by the dungeon,' Swallow said. 'It's your reward for helping us.'

Shaggy the Wild Cat purred and ate and purred and ate all through the night.

About the Author

David Thomson was born in Quetta in 1914. Much of his childhood was spent in the country, in a Derbyshire village and at Nairn, on the Moray Firth in Scotland, where his grandparents lived. As a boy he spent most of his time helping on a farm. He did a milk-round every morning with a pony and cart in the old part of Nairn, where the fishermen live.

After leaving Oxford he took a job in a remote part of Ireland and stayed almost ten years. His experiences there inspired two of his books *The People of the Sea* (about seals and their legends) and *Woodbrook*, the story of the farm where he worked. As a BBC producer he first worked on *Country Magazine* and has written and produced many folklore programmes, including a series called *The Irish Storyteller*. He has also done documentary work for the BBC in Lappland and for UNESCO in Liberia and Turkey.

Danny Fox and *Danny Fox Meets a Stranger* were his first books for children.

Some Other Young Puffins

BANDICOOT AND HIS FRIENDS
Violet Philpott

Lion promised his friends a surprise when he came home from India, but no one expected anything half as nice as friendly funny, furry little Bandicoot, who was so kind and clever when any of his friends were in trouble.

ADVENTURES OF SAM PIG
Alison Uttley

Ten funny and magical stories about Alison Uttley's best-loved creation. For children of five to nine.

LITTLE BEAR'S FEATHER and RUN FOR HOME
Evelyn Davies

Two separate stories on similar themes: Little Bear is a Red Indian Chief's son, Matthew, the child of English settlers in Red Indian territory. They both have a dream and both find they must be brave in an unexpected way to realize it.

THE ADVENTURES OF UNCLE LUBIN

W. Heath Robinson

The amazing adventures of good old Uncle Lubin in his search for his little nephew, Peter, who has been stolen by the wicked Bag-bird. With the author's own unforgettable illustrations.

DAVID AND HIS GRANDFATHER

Pamela Rogers

Three long stories about David and his kind, friendly Grandfather, who participates in all his secret schemes.

JACKO AND OTHER STORIES

Jean Sutcliffe

Stories about pets and people by an expert who is really in touch with young children – the creator of the *Listen With Mother* programme.

THE OWL WHO WAS AFRAID OF THE DARK

Jill Tomlinson

Being afraid of the dark has its problems, especially when you're a baby owl, but Plop comes to learn that the dark can be exciting, fun, beautiful and a lot else besides.